The Engraver

The Engraver

Hermann Stehr

K A Nitz
ALBANY, NEW ZEALAND

Der Graveur was first published
in *Auf Leben und Tod* 1898

Revised Printing 2019

ISBN: 978-0-473-21205-6

National Library of New Zealand Cataloguing-
in-Publication Data

Stehr, Hermann, 1864-1940.
Graveur. German
The engraver / by Hermann Stehr ; translated
by Kerry Nitz.
ISBN 978-0-473-21205-6
l. Nitz, Kerry, 1971- ll. Title
833.912—dc 22

There is a very life in our despair,
Vitality of poison, — a quick root
Which feeds these deadly branches; for it were
As nothing did we die; but life will suit
Itself to Sorrow's most detested fruit,
Like to the apples on the Dead Sea shore,
All ashes to the taste: ...

Lord Byron — Childe Harold's Pilgrimage,
Canto 3, XXXIV

The Engraver

"Likewise, what use is it working all day if you hang about all evening in taverns? Evening! — ha, ha! — you've never heard the clock at home strike eleven. The devil too, where are you running to with your nose to the ground like a mutt that has lost the trail? What you're looking for you surely won't find anymore! He who pours his business down his throat ... But to the knackers, precisely! — Don't you see, here's the main road, that is the forest, maples on left and right, that is the ditch — but you know that, of course — hm — if it goes on like this it'll be your retirement home!"

The speaker, a man of medium build with a brown beard and wide hat, stopped, held his hand over his eyes, and then looked into the valley which sloped away from his feet.

The evening sun was glowing behind the mountains. Its golden rays were flickering over the back of the nearby range. The range lay already veiled before him in the evening gloaming. Here and there on its slopes lights flickered. To his astonished eyes they seemed to wander back and forth, flickering. But the observer knew the mountain was farmed to the top.

"Odd," he opened his compressed lips, "that people know exactly when it becomes night. At that moment each one lights his lamp. But when the night lifts rarely does an eyelid."

His grey eyes, still watching intently, were getting tired, the lids sinking. The lines of his face, which with the words to his companion had furrowed hard into his cheeks, were now disappearing. His countenance was becoming quiet, solemn, like that of a man hearing a distant bell tolling or having beautiful thoughts and dreams.

After a few minutes of quiet thought he stroked his face and asked, turning energetically to go, "And what do you want to do now?"

His companion tore his face from the ground. The teeth of his upper jaw had buried themselves in his fleshy lower lip, his facial muscles still twitched at the sides in anger. But then he turned his face fully towards his questioner and — instantly friendliness flung open his lips and rolled them full and sensual, his squarely cleft chin fell into boundless good humour and embedded itself in the softening fat of his face.

"What to do? — simple, simple! — You see, brother Joseph ..."

The Engraver

He stopped, spread his short, fat legs, and leant back on his gnarled stick, pushed back his wide-brimmed hat, and fixed his stationary companion firmly in the eye. Something new was going through his head — something distant and strange, but interesting. He pulled himself together.

"Simple, simple! Craftwork is no more, despite the guild's mumbo-jumbo. Nonsense, I say to you, it's utter nonsense! It's all disappearing! Just wait a few years and our fat colleagues will be just like me. Who is to blame? Bismarck who ...", he flinched at the word on his tongue, and glanced around with concern, "who, with his trade barriers, his pig ban, his, who knows what, knackered all the butchers. Knackered, I say to you!"

He raised his stick.

"I'm a victim of politics, nothing more. I've been tearing my hair out lately. When I say to my assistant, 'Go and fetch a pig, but a fat one, a bacon pig, God damn!', in the evening he returns hard of breath, as if he had run around the world, and brings a pig, a little pig — so — so —".

He stoops, and almost touches the ground with his hand, but it is pointless, it is pitch dark.

"So — oh God, its ears hardly look up from the trough and a hundred and fifty marks — a pound and seventy pennies. Well, and who buys it? The worker? He has no money, you have to laugh,

laugh ... The official? Well yes, but, 'Only without bones, my pay is low and everything is expensive, dear Mr Schramm!' and with that his wife makes a pitiful face. You can't withstand that, I couldn't. Lord, why was I so soft-hearted and lent six marks, nine, twenty and so on and so on ... and then it is gone and it ... ha, ha! I am a victim of politics, nothing more! What am I going to do? You see, dear brother — you know father always said when August ..."

"Oh, if father were still alive! Lucky for him that he is dead!"

The speaker seemed not to have heard.

"Our father poor devil", he murmured and then a cordially upbeat, fervid zest for action quivered in his exhausted voice, "I have already made plans for when it starts to fall apart. When everything is ironed out I am still left with about three hundred marks. With that I can buy a horse and cart, hang out my shingle and do business with cattle, pigs, etc, etc. I understand buying like Moses. With little pigs you tear the clothes from your own body. The business has to go. But I'm not buying them from the gentlemen who feed themselves richly on the class politics of Prince Bismarck. I'd rather go collect rags. Over in Bohemia the pigs are almost for free, you kill half the litter. Four guilders for a pair, I tell you, clean as. You drink a few bottles of brew with the taxmen, say good night, and leave a five mark note in their hand. I tell you, they're struck blind then. I know the deal."

"And if they make you trade in contraband?"

"Idiot", the small man was thinking and wanted to shake with laughter.

"On that I have no worries. — Over there each pair of pigs costs four guilders. That is about seven marks, and here I don't sell them for less than fifty marks, making at least thirty five marks straight profit. If in three years I don't get back everything that I have lost, then call me Hans, Hans I say!"

It seemed to the thoughtful one walking along that despondency had not seized the bankrupt one. But the way in which he developed his schemes, the wild, dizzying, the blind fabric of his plans suggested the spirit from which his previous entrepreneurial drive had flowed. He thought he could smell it, and stuck closer to the side of his brother.

He, however, was storming along, raising his stick more and more vigorously. His thoughts churned through his soul just the same.

Then two years later — how fast two years go — four horses were being kept. A house in Neurode ... on the Ring, of course ... from the baker Krause ... admittedly, he wanted to be compensated entirely with gold. — But, my God! After two, three years, what is eight thousand marks to me then when the business is going like so?

It is definite, it must be so.

... and then, of course, I won't travel myself anymore. It will — in place and position — be accomplished let's say with five to six thousand pieces. The merchant handles the goods. My God, the poor sucker will also want to have something.

Division of labour, that is the secret.

He had also divided the labour up to now, right to the point where there was only the appearance of hard work. That is the secret.

He had found the key to the puzzle of modern times, in which everything is the result of lust, hunger, anger and gluttony, gloom and disgust.

Titles rained on him — city father, orphan's counsel ... dammit, and did you, you fat nosed, filing moth, Lord Mayor, understand then that I am no longer the unscrupulous one who left his family stranded?

This future!

He stopped, raised his head, and stared into the night. The images of his imagination danced colourfully, no, beautifully past him. The firs were whispering over him in such a typically mysterious way. The austere melody gave the visions flying around him spirit and heart. Now the moon was climbing through the branches. It rolled up, a glowing ember like his inner plans.

They gradually went out in front of him and in him. But the lustful feeling remained. He had forgotten that he was homeless, a beggar, and destitute. The hard times of his struggles lay behind him. He sampled the blessings of his inner life, he sipped joy.

That is life!

"That demands a slug", suddenly the old drinking song mechanically hummed through his head like a solemn hymn. He pulled the bottle from his side pocket, held it up to the moonlight, and shook the contents. The schnaps swirled. He looked at his brother through the liquid — hunchbacked, knotted together, he ran about like a dwarf, flapping his legs ridiculously. Of course, he was an ant, he could only scratch, glean, and be stingy. But his poor skull had never concocted an enterprising, massive thought. In that respect he was a different fellow.

That all flew like an arrow through his head.

Then the schnaps vanished in one pull. He corked the bottle slowly. A dignified calm settled over him. His thoughts had gainfully concluded their serious lifespan. He viewed with reflective emotion his bankruptcy, which seemed to be pushed far, far behind him into the unreal. He observed himself full of admiration, he who had survived such difficulty and was now one of the most ostracised.

He felt in a mood in which every doubt, every interjection, even every well-intended piece of advice made him gruff, hard, spiteful, rude, could even incense him enormously.

In such moments he, the otherwise good-tempered but sanguine crank, had ill-treated his wife and children, clobbered his assistants with his stick, smashed glasses on the heads of the barmen, and thrown his money around wantonly by the handful.

The animated smile vanished from his face. He strode on with back straight. He didn't need to grovel.

"I see already that your audacity and your plans", his brother began in a serious sounding tone, "are all hogwash."

"Everyone knows his business best. When I tell you ..."

"We'll let that be," he interrupted, "that comes later, if it comes at all."

"What are you saying to me? You understand as much about my business as a calf about egg-laying!"

"When does the contract expire? How long does your family still have lodging?"

The butcher ground his teeth over such 'bagatelles'. Now, when there are other burning questions, the stub nose comes out with such lousy trifles! Just wait!

"The 32nd January past!", he growled with suppressed laughter.

"I'm asking because of your children. I regret them having such a father."

"Amen!", mocked the small man.

"Your paternal love, your entire humanity is drowned in booze. That's why you are incapable of any generosity. And do I deserve to be treated by you like this? Do you think that I will give you the thousand marks that I won myself through hard work and that you wasted so frivolously?"

"Then take my wife, my children! My wife, yes, yes, you are single! You have the hand here, work it off! You — you — altar bread eater!"

He was foaming with fury.

The road turned to the north-west. They entered a narrow cutting leading down into the valley. The butcher was walking on the righthand edge. The engraver was walking in the low depression of the stony road. The edges on both sides rose up to his hips. He now strafed the tottering walker next to and above him with a contemptuous look.

"Wretch!", erupted from his lips.

The other one didn't hear it. He was taking care not to fall off the edge. He was swearing and ranting. Over what, he wasn't conscious of. Then he was hushed suddenly by the certainty in his head that his brother despised him, was ashamed of him.

"You, my God — cuckoo!"

He stopped and turned to him. With sarcastic, bitter laughter it fell raw and broken from his lips, "I have no money ... Of course I have to go with you ... But I don't want to sleep at your place. God forbid me ... I still have enough life in me to understand that a beggar belongs by the door — although he is human too — and would be a brother. I'll go to the glass factory and lay myself on the ash heaps. It's warm there. If someone were to ask me ... but, who will ask me? ... They know me and will let me be. I am, of course, the brother of Mr Engraver and Mr Engraver has the rights to this gentleman, that is, the engraver has his rights continually in the wallet of the gentleman. Mr Engraver is a religious gouger whose gentle 'Our Father' face doesn't make the the devil overlook that he cheated his brother of a thousand marks of his inheritance, of the same thousand marks that he then nobly lent him."

"Ha, ha! You holy thief!"

He spat at the pale, painfully cold face of the man standing below him, and then staggered backwards from the edge crashing through branches to the ground.

The engraver grasped at his heart. The disappointment was clenching it. That then, he thought, after all your worry, your heartache over him? Everything he had done for him surged up in his memory. He had lent him his capital for starting his business so that he was able to offer competition. Then, when his brother's passions were shaking its barely established existence, he had helped a much as he could. He had surrendered everything. His family's honour should not be trampled underfoot. In the calamitous period before the business's bankruptcy, all the worries, all the heartache had rested on his shoulders. He was adviser, comforter, and support for his desperate sister-in-law, a father to the children. In the generosity of the deed itself he had sought and found his thanks and reward. The rumours that he cheated his brother to keep the 'rabble' afloat hardly touched him.

He had been at peace, cheerfully serious as only a pure disposition is able to be.

Now, however, this drunkard was standing up against him and laughing rawly at his help. Now his brother, for whom he'd done everything, was throwing base accusations at him.

That's why he felt defeated. He was one of those slow-moving, deep characters who are not able to feel and think anything superficially, who at the first surprise stride on in unworldly silence for days, even weeks, pondering, planning and conjecturing, and automatically never jumping to a conclusion by which the business might be subjected to fate or wrenched away by accident.

Thus he also stood for a long time now in sombre thought. Finally his brooding resolved itself into the muffled cry, "So he is a dishonourable man, my brother!" –

He winced as his own words struck his ears.

"Whaaat doo, do you ...", the drunk laboured upwards just barely.

"Wait," he shrieked in bestial fury, "wait, I want to drink to you, that you should think of the rags your whole life long!" He tore the schnaps bottle from his side pocket, and swung it over his head.

The engraver watched with cold indifference.

Suddenly a glowing red fireball exploded before his eyes. At the same time a heavy blow met his forehead. His brother's shadow grew quick as an arrow to a dizzying height and daunting breadth. The roaring in his ears got stronger and stronger. The night waltzed around him with whispering wingbeats. Meanwhile, from miles away, came the cry, "Rogue — cheat — whore chaser!"

Cold fright raced through his body. Instinct tears him into defending himself. He raises his arms, flailing around madly, weakly. His consciousness is dying away. He just felt soft, weakening blows rain down on his head. From each blow a voluptuous, weary warmth streams over his face and through his body. Sheaves of fire flicker before him. They become paler and paler. — Now he feels himself rising quick as the wind, screaming. His consciousness is returning once more. It is to him as though his head was butting up against the heavens. He opens his eyes, and sees the blood red moon close in front of him, and in fear he stretches his hand out at it to clutch it to himself.

But the blackest night is already rushing up. Suddenly it pulls him into the depths. –

In the morning passersby found the unconscious man streaming with blood on the road.

The Engraver

The engraver feels himself being carried by something. It flies, it rolls, tottering uncertainly like a ship. Now it looks like a ball, now like a wide, dark expanse sinking and rising in flight.

However, he has the feeling that he must go away — where? — far — far –

Now the expanse suddenly hunches and puts him down. What had been under him now draws in front of him. He is separated from it, but the feeling still remains that he must go far, far away. He directs his eyes steadily onto the rolling dark balls in front of him — slowly they stretch out into two legs like giant spruce trees. A rectangular trunk is slowly growing now, and a head whose weather beaten face was chiseled as though from stone. Haze forms an umbra around it entirely, especially the face. It condenses, it dissolves. As it comes and goes, grows and vanishes, now entices, now threatens, the face seems to also change its expression. But it also only seems the same. In truth it remains grey, stony, stiff and dead, and the changes fly over it like storm clouds, like smiling light.

Now it looks like a devil's face, smiling sweetly, remorselessly genial, odiously enticing. He is afraid, and wants to hide, but haze is everywhere, and he is entirely alone, and — — — must not hesitate ... and with beading sweat of fear on his brow he flees far from the terrible sight ... far ... as it rolls its eyes glowering. Then its head flips — the inside becomes the outside as though thoughts are becoming tangible image ... oh, and what an image!

The face of Lear, the mad king — the high, white forehead, the restlessly wandering and rigid grey eyes, the mouth warped painfully by eternally hidden torment and despair, the unmoving bloodless lips. But a sigh and whimper break through the air. Nothing is heard, and yet it courses through the engraver like an icy shower through his soul.

It climbs to a breathless, mortal fear when he notices that the man is not walking away from him anymore but heading towards him. And suddenly he realises with distress that the forward pull which governs him is increasing.

Now he is flying like the wind. He shivers full of angst, and yet the heavy pull feels like sweetness. Now he is feeling the grim arms laying themselves slowly around his body, the stone-cold forehead pressing tighter and tighter against his own. The restlessly wandering, soul-orphaned eyes are boring into his soul.

He feels his life ebbing away, slowly — slowly — there into the dead, empty eyes — but they remain dead.

Then he feels that in the most secret workshop of his being something clinging, bearing down, oppressive is falling.

He has the feeling of an inner resurrection.

The cold, the death, the breathless cheeks, the stiffening is going away, and he is feeling warmth, life, fire shooting inwards and tingling through his body. At the same time he is climbing upwards as though an inner strength is raising him. He still has his eyes closed in fear. But it is skimming over his skin soft and pleasant — it is light! — — —

He feels it and boldly opens his eyes, riveting them tightly to the terrible image which is still clasping hold of him. Gradually the grip loosens, the face less distinct, paler.

At last he feels only a weak angst, sees only a gentle, grey haze before his eyes, before his soul.

However, he is flying upwards, lighter — faster — more fervently.

Then he awakes and glances around. –

Above him red flowers are blooming. He turns. The sunlight floods through the window in broad, golden stripes. On the wall he sees a man and a woman. They are smiling. They are greeting him, these good people. Only who can they be? He would like to go towards them, but he is feeling so weak he can only confusedly wish. Only who are they, these good people?

It sounds so sweet, so happy that his heart skips a beat. He is drunk on the infatuating tone. He strains to recognise who and what it is!

Oh!

It is old Therese, it is his room, the picture on the wall, the couple in the forest and — he — will not die!

The red flowers ... the golden light ... the laughing faces ... life! ... life!

He smiles blissfully. —

Yet already it is beginning to whirl around him, everything is dancing colourfully and condensing into the night which lays itself on, over, and in him.

With the weak cry, "Oh!", he sinks back into unconsciousness.

Then the old woman starts with fear, walks around, and plonks down the glass in which she was stirring a liquid. The clink rips the fevered man once more into consciousness.

He looks at the old woman who has hurried to the side of his bed — smiles weakly, and closes his eyes, ejaculating incomprehensible sounds.

"Jesus, Maria and all the holy angels! Mr Joseph, dearest Mr Schramm! Do you know me? I am your old, faithful Therese, dear Mr Joseph!"

But, lying in fever, he did not hear her.

"Six days already now", murmured the old woman, glancing into the courtyard where ragged boys scrapped. She was staring like one who wants to escape an inner pain, seeking and finding something distracting, and soon seeing in everything only the pale face of the deep mental suffering from which she wished to flee. She sighed deeply and with a sob, "He is not my child, but if I left I would have to spit at myself. No — no!" she encouraged herself in her fortitude. "... and then straightaway something wholesome ... only what did the doctor say ..."

He will wake up again.

She went on tiptoes to his bed, and looked fixedly at the pale patient whose fever-dry lips moved spasmodically. She looked ceaselessly at him, with a wishfulness and love like a gardener watching a laboriously tended plant whose flowering he is expecting — he imagines the flower, counts the petals in his mind's eye, fancies he can smell the scent, and hears himself already with ardent words delightedly telling his wife or every third person the happy news. So too did she recall to her memory the quickly flown smile of his reawakening, imagined the pale motionless face smiling, and scolded herself as 'a clumsy thing' because of the glass. Her intention was only to make him roll over again. Then she pondered the words she would say to him when he awoke again.

It must have been something jovial, for she twisted her mouth into a broad, ungainly smile. But her blue-grey eyes looked so blissfully at him that her face would have matched a happy child's if the creases had not been there.

And she would tell the doctor such and such. He had done such and such. I stood there and so on, exactly, for "the doctor must know everything exactly, otherwise he will never come to rights."

With these thoughts of her wordy tale she all of a sudden became hasty and animated. She performed all the actions she wanted to mention, folded her hands one over the other repeatedly, distressed, regretful, helpless. She let the spirit of her words flitter over her face, and in between pulled and plucked at the patient's bedcover in distressed anxiousness. She adjusted his head bandage, and brushed the faded cheeks of the 'poor fellow' with her rough, hard hand.

Then the door opened, and the doctor entered.

Therese turned around so hastily that the little table was shaken and the medicine bottle clinked.

"Hello, doctor", she stammered like a child caught in the act.

"Hello, Therese", his tongue rubbed over his teeth. "Now, how is he? better? awake? groggy? still in fever? hm, hm."

He took the patient's limply hanging hand, and felt the pulse, scrutinising him attentively. He obviously did not expect an answer to his quick-fire questions.

"Hm, hm, ... when did he come around? how long ago?" Therese goggled at him speechlessly, and in her admiration initially forgot her beautifully studied tale. Then, however, the locks of her eloquence broke.

The doctor bore it with a smile which looked like a vexed grimace. He never smiled any differently.

"It won't be long," he firmly interrupted in the end, "and the patient will wake up again. I will prescribe him something for strengthening and stimulating his appetite. He might have lost his speech. But I hope he'll get completely well again with peace and careful, restful treatment. Above all, Therese, avoid all allusions to his brother and his misfortune, otherwise ..."

"But ..." he broke off roughly, and thought further, that won't work. What's the use of telling her everything? She won't understand.

"Behave around him as though he's a child."

"Jesus, Jesus! my God! dumb! you're not saying?" she cried.

It should have sounded hushed, but it rang out across the room like a painful cry.

"Oh!", came distended and flat from the patient's bed.

The doctor hurried to him.

"Now, Mr Schramm, had a good sleep? That's nice. Good morning! Do you have a headache?"

He took the patient's hand which he had relinquished, contemplated him kindly and smiled. But his smile was repellent to watch. It was as though vengeful schadenfreude was battling weakly on his face with tearful rage. He couldn't smile any other way.

To begin with the patient smiled like a six week old child, awkward, empty and weak.

Suddenly, however, he looked terrified and full of fear.

A gurgling sound full of despair came from his lips. The doctor walked away, and the engraver, paralysed with terror, riveted his wide-open eyes firmly on something which seemed to float in the air before him.

Bit by bit the horror disappears from his features, and his eyes close as though fatigued. Still whispering, the doctor gives the old woman a few instructions, and then slips out noiselessly.

Therese sighs, and stands for a long time sunk in anguish. Then she goes and mixes up a drink, and offers it to the patient.

He shuts his eyes, and smiles again that mute, empty, weak smile. Then he slurps the liquid offered to him.

Therese turns hastily, and stifles a sob. She would like to stay and talk, and console him, but she mustn't. Yet she isn't able to look at the helpless one without venting her anguish. She walks softly out the door. Outside she creeps down the creaking stairs wringing her hands and crying bitterly in her apron.

Meanwhile Schramm was lying there with wide-open eyes. They glided curiously and hastily over the entire room, clinging delightedly to each object for a while.

He recognised every item — the red flowers on the bedcover, the picture on the wall, the flower table in the corner, the cage with the canary on the cabinet, outside the mountains, sky, sun, clouds, and houses. He had the feeling of having wandered far, far away and now returned. Yet, of where he had been, of the times and of the circumstances of the journey, of that he had no consciousness. A distant land lay in him — mountains, rivers, sky, forests, and houses. Everything in a white, alluring spring dawn, but everything without life, without end, without aim, without reference to one another. He didn't reach this mute world inside him by reflection but rather it spread out, grew and became clearer with the increasing number of objects that his senses perceived. This world didn't lie behind him either. His soul was surrounded by it. He had lost every idea of the passage of time.

If a new object met his senses then he felt a warm, voluptuous swelling in and out within himself, as it were, flooding towards the thing whose image passed down into his soul and there raised up from the white, alluring spring dawn its copy, which had long rested there, though extinguished, buried. He constantly had a feeling of satisfaction then, of being confident, even a certain childish pride, if one, because our language lacks the right words for this state, wants to superimpose the complex or lofty for the simple or lower. It was a specific animal-like, organic wantonness which configured itself from the accord and harmony of the consequences of the senses rummaging in such various ways. His recognition of the outside world had collected many likenesses by the method a small child uses to collect experiences, i.e. images. But the effect, the state of his soul issuing from it, was very different. Whilst in the soul of a small child restless zeal and addiction to experience emerges from the elation of independent discovery, from the reflection of the outer world in his inner world, a solemn, satiated, contented joy wove itself around Schramm's life. However, he felt this joy not so much in his heart and soul, but rather as complacency spreading throughout his entire body. He tasted it with his tongue. It was as though he felt it soft and soothing when he rubbed his hands together.

His joy was evoked by the recognition of the relationship or similarity of physical things with each other and with the internal images entering into his spiritual visibility in ever greater number and clarity — similarities in form, colour, guise, dimensions and movement. It was in a word an indirect and also not clearly conscious joy over having found himself unchanged after he had travelled far, so far.

What delighted him the most was that, for example, he heard the song of the canary muffled for a long time, lingering in a peculiar tone colouring inside him, colours which continued to glow dreamlike after their demise, and he saw objects moving restlessly. Then his senses turned their powers as it were inwards, and he observed rapt for hours the multi-coloured, soulless kaleidoscope of his dead inner life. —

In particular, he had the idea that what he saw and heard had been seen and heard often, had been familiar to him. But this memory was only tied to sensually perceptible properties, even excluding any idea of the passage of time. People of his close acquaintance also exercised nothing more than a mere sense stimulus at first. Their words were only echos to him and they irritated his sensitive nerves in a familiar manner. He was in a position to differentiate the tones and the nuances of voices, but only in so far as the different sounds, now empty, dispirited, without emotional powers of animation, had previously flooded through his consciousness. —

To foreign, unfamiliar tones, objects and faces he behaved bluntly and indifferently, merely because they did not call forth inner, organic shadows of memory.

His soul thus reposed for weeks between beastly night and clear, well-lit consciousness, in the dawning of a spiritual doze. –

The Engraver

Many days and nights passed. Schramm spent them in sleeping, eating, and contemplation. Gradually he became stronger. Already he was allowed to sit in a chair for hours, and take a few steps around the room on the arm of the old woman.

His inner being was changing.

It was like nature in winter when the sun creeps across the sky with its eyes closed like a sleepwalker, with a pale, drowsy look. The things on earth are standing there alone and trapped, each one at the same time avoiding and being moved by its own cold, heavy anguish and gloom. The wonderful, natural trait of sympathy between them all is torn apart, and likewise death, in which everything shivers, cannot unite them.

The weeping willow stands bowed over the stream. Its crown dithers like a head numbed with pain, and if a light breeze moves it then it swings its long, limp switchs whimpering as though it was flagellating its scrawny body in dull, nameless torment. The stream boils and bubbles in grief, the firs grumble and groan in grim misery. The stone kicked off the path cries out shrill and sharp like the alienated poor thrown into the gutter by hard heartedness.

But everything bears the same death alone, forgotten and timid.

But then if in March the snow thaws, the ice melts, the brown waves roll booming, the happy sky looks down curiously from torn clouds with soulful, deep-blue eyes, and the sun strolls in ever more adventurous arcs in its childish, ripening girl's beauty, so auspiciously, so alluringly, so coyly veiling her burgeoning charms; then the foreboding of death and loneliness breaks. A wonderful, invisible life, inclination and wishfulness adheres and sputters between things. A mute jubilation rests on the closed lips of the tree buds while the tree stretches its branches to the heavens in the joy of reunion.

Everything hustles and struggles for the expression of a new life of harmony and sweet affiliation.

The observant human spirit sees the living things fettered to the earth toiling to embrace him, to tell him something, to open the base of their being, to propagate. He broods and looks for ideas and concepts, for clarity and only ever raises himself to the enchanted, adoring, vague exclamation.

The Engraver

The same metamorphosis had taken place in Schramm's soul. He stood for the second time in a spiritual early spring.

He sat in a chair, his head leaning back wearily. His eyes were half closed, his mouth slightly open. Over his entire face lay a heavenly rapture, heightened by the sickly paleness in his expression.

The rays of the rising sun were spreading out their trembling multi-coloured fan. Glittering bands came and went on the yellow cabinet in the corner. In the flower table's clutter of plants the light dissolved dreamlike into its colours. The goldfish swam as though in the red sky, and one didn't know whether the sparkling water was making the fish through condensation or whether the goldfish were dissolving into their sparkling element.

The brass plate of the pendulum swung in garrulous regularity from the sunshine to the shadows. It looked like an eye which, always bedazzled and closed by the sun, opened again and again like a rotund dwarf who was restlessly hauling the sunshine on his back into the night to light his home.

The canary fluttered with wistful call towards the light of freedom.

Outside the trees were rustling, the birds singing, and the monotonous hum of the main road drifted into his room.

His soul was opening with an austere complacency to the flow of new sounds and colours assiduously collected by his senses.

Suddenly he realised that the cabinet, unlike the other objects, was of the form of a prism. He noticed the chink of the lock on its door, the ornaments, the drawer and the short feet. It seemed like a puzzle to him, like a fairy tale. The question "why?" didn't occur to him, around the cabinet floated a multi-coloured animated life only visible to him. He heard it knocking around the cabinet, groaning, screeching, hissing, sputtering, falling ... but distant, muffled, vague. People, things, colours, experiences rose up and slipped away in a hazy mist or piece by piece.

On the wall it was also becoming vivid. The pattern was fading. He saw an image vaguely scurrying through his memory. He heard disjointed words: ... wants ... blue ... base pattern ... well yes! ... ha ...

The oven crumbled away, it rumbled, beat dully, threw something down. Then he heard it — hearth ... good heating ... open ... good.

A face rose up in his soul, and quickly died away.

His memory was working itself out of the frenzy and into clarity. The spirit of the past began to draw into the recovered sensual perceptions, either flattened and incoherent or full and clear but quickly disappearing.

The Engraver

The circle of experiences, which tied itself to every piece of his belongings or the things outside, lent each its own spiritual face on whose tormented lips words, concepts, facts, whole scenes struggled out, became an undertone, became silent again and finally as it were only came into view by the gesture of speaking. The same feeling of dissatisfaction ruled Schramm's soul, the same fearful, vexed brooding which engages with any almost-familiar face he sees. He searches for the name, broods, broods, sees in the meantime scenes in dreamlike clarity, is reminded of conversations which seemed to be tied to this person and continues to brood without achieving a clear recollection.

Schramm pondered, pondered passionately with throbbing chest, glowing eyes, thumping temples, firmly shut lips. It drove him to the suddenly dawning conviction, more sensed than anything, that he must find clarity otherwise his life would be miserable.

He thought about it full of fear.

As if with sharp vulture talons his eyes grasped at the images which danced around him, rising up and dying away. If he caught them and riveted his searching gaze on them, they dissolved or transformed into other images never seen before, which his eyes chased after anew, as though lusting for them, until they again stood restless and maddened before the insubstantial.

Sweat was already pearling on the patient's brow, and still no scene, no word, no thing emerged into clarity from the colours, images, things, tones and noises.

His fearful longing was already sinking into painful despondency as he saw the cabinet door merge into his memory. A woman's image emerged clear and sharp out of the dark background. She turned her back to Schramm and hung something up. It was so lucid and clear that the thought of an illusion didn't occur to him. With held breath, throbbing heart and nameless rapture in his wide-open eyes he stared at the image, like a thinker at an idea finally found, like an inventor at the model he saw so often in his dreams.

Now the image was turning towards him, and turning her lively, kindly smiling face to him.

"Oh God, oh yes, it is my sister, of course", he cried, clapping his hands together delightedly.

The old woman started in fright. She heard Schramm exhale a dull, overly loud gurgling sound.

She saw suddenly the horror that was slowly disfiguring his features. His face assumed the same desperately frightened expression as when he perceived the doctor's sneering smile after returning to consciousness. His eyes were fixed rigidly on something floating in the air in front of him.

The Engraver

Immediately after the cry, probably because of the mental exertion, Schramm had seen the more and more colourful and increasingly clear world of his memory collapse as though kicked into a whir of little pieces. The same sombre shadows then drew across his soul and now titanic threatening faces were swelling up. The feverish dream in which he had risen to consciousness stretched out through him again with its horrific images and emotions.

A terrible fear, which seemed to have slept in him for a long time, numbed as it were, struggling for consciousness, sprang up in his heart and rolled shivering through all his limbs.

... Then the countenance of the dream transformed itself. A devil's face stared at him, smiling sweetly, remorselessly mild, odiously alluring.

In the same moment the doctor enters. He is in deep thought, lays aside his hat and stick, strides mechanically to Schramm, smiles his strange smile, offers him his hand, and only then fixes his eyes fully on the motionless patient.

Schramm springs up, backs away horrified, madly makes motions of fending off with his arms, all the while emitting gurgled cries for help.

The sneering smile petrifies on the lips of the doctor. Thoughts pass through his mind — he is crazy, if you flee then you are lost, he will spring at you and str...

He goes heartily to the retreating Schramm, smiling desperately, "What's wrong? ... Head ... ache ... l–lie — down — in — bed ...", he stuttered softly.

Schramm shrank back.

"There it is! Oh, it is coming, it is coming nearer, the face of Satan!", the searing dread cried out on him.

He has reached the wall, and cannot go any further. They both drill their eyes into one another.

Agonising minutes elapse slowly like years.

In the third storey of the workers' barracks which Schramm inhabited a rumbling rose above them. A muffled whirl of voices sounds through the ceiling. The door in a room above is ripped crashing from its hinges. One hears a jumble of cursing, harsh and drunken laughter, bumps and dragging sounds. Now a load is rolling down fast and heavy. Painful silence follows. Then it is as though someone were rising slowly and uncertainly from a fall. Something smashes into the door of Schramm's room, then one hears a deep, masculine voice grumbling and groaning in grim fury.

At this sign of life from below, whinnying laughter reverberates from the floor above.

"Bones like a rubber man!"

The Engraver

Frenetic cheering rewards this jest.

Then the one thrown down rises fizzing with fury, "What, you — you — rogue, cheat, whore chaser."

This ejaculation is also heard in Schramm's room. It strikes the engraver like a thunderclap. Bright light shoots through his soul like lightning. The dreamlike face, and the heavy cloud of fear and half consciousness abruptly flee. The world of his surroundings, with all that he saw, thought and experienced in it, bears down on him, cold and vulgar. But he feels everything like a painful stab straight to his heart.

He springs up, and — in the next moment sinks down inwardly broken.

For clearer and more precisely than every thing before, the memory rises of the narrow cutting. It grows quickly in him like a poisonous plant, it spreads its grim branches over all the images of his memory. It stands within him in the full sunlight of perfect consciousness. The rest steps more or less into a hazy twilight, pushed away, overrun or timidly retreating! –

The staggering shadow of his brother grows lightning quick to dizzying height and daunting breadth. The bottle flashing in the blood-red moonlight circles and glints like the murderous eyes of a predator. The cry of impotent fury swims from an infinite distance muffled on trembling wings into his breast — rogue, cheat, whore chaser! It digs and drills into him like a corrosive venom.

His pure, deeply moral character twitches lifelessly under the disgraceful prohibition of suspicion by his brother.

He stands dispirited for a long time, his head resting on his chest, his eyes closed.

Then he feels it boiling up hot as embers inside, storming, roaring and thrusting like a wave of fire. The peace and order of his entire organism is torn up. It ferments and blusters in him like a revolution. Thoughts and sensations, feeling, passion and strength of will battle, balled up in a turbid, shapeless mass. His heart pounded against his chest like heavy crushing blows, but mad and irregular.

It is the throes of his mild, contemplative, seriously affectionate soul which refuses to accept the birth of a dark passion, like the earth sown with flowers refusing to accept the fuming volcano which rumples its inner life and threatens its mirth.

Suddenly the vague surging and foaming clenches into the gorgon face of fury, into passionate rage and loathing.

Every nerve, every fibre, every feeling, every sensation is gifted a language. Like a call for help, like an accusation, he cries out inwardly,

"What, me a rogue, me a cheat? me?!"

The Engraver

And the mute, dying echo of passion runs as a tremor through his tensed muscles. –

Schramm then feels so empty, so cold, so forsaken, wretched and exposed by everything and everyone in the world, like a castaway thrown by the waves onto an inhospitable, deserted, rocky beach.

"Oh God!" he calls imploringly, sitting down on the edge of the bed and lapsing into dull brooding.

Sitting distraught and broken like the forsaken, defiled maiden; like the man who betrayed his friend; like the child who disowned his parents; like the researcher who after a life of thinking sees his system dissolving into a conceited phantom.

The sun rises and sets, the market fills and empties, the flowers bloom, the stream of people rushes and glides colourfully and varyingly past them.

However, they look at everything indifferently, with a weak, dispirited smile on pale lips. And in them there is no hope, no belief, neither love nor hate, neither pain nor joy, empty, empty, they are turning to stone from the inside out.

Everything is over until death!

Oh, were it so, foolish, blind man-child! –

The Engraver

The remaining memory of his past receded before the remembered image of the scene in the narrow cutting and all the experiences, thoughts and feelings connected with it, and this urged his thinking with irresistible force to the sombre events of the recent past. It happened though that during the ascendancy of his illness his spirit had been troubled by strength and independence, that he had further subdued the quick changes and surges of his recovering organism, that the more sensitive states were becoming more and more common, whilst generosity, meekness, conciliatory leniency and all the higher, absolutely spiritual stirrings were less and less frequently in excess.

Otherwise he had not placed highly the value of his selfless worries for the welfare of his brother and his unhappy family, had known and wanted no other compensation than the satisfaction and peace which the good deed offered him. Now, however, he was suddenly becoming conceited over his character and his conduct.

"He isn't worth my little finger and calls me a rogue? Who would treat me so? Not one in a thousand!", were the thoughts that constantly engaged him.

His weak state, and the pains which the wounds were causing his head, darkened his brother's vicious behaviour into the blackest crime, and he saw himself as a martyr.

He liked to linger with these thoughts especially. He drew new indignation from them when his enfeebled spirit wanted to turn away dull and indifferent.

The inability of being able to communicate with others internalised his anger more and more. In the end he only lived in his fury. He sent himself to sleep with it, rolled it through his soul in chilling dream images and found each morning a new side that he had not yet seen and reflected upon.

Once he raised himself from his bed. It was late morning. Old Therese placed his breakfast on the little table by the bed.

"You've slept a long time, Mr Josef. It is 10 o'clock. Well, I am just happy you're almost well again. Sleeping is half sustenance. Children and sick people must sleep a lot. How did you dream?"

Schramm looked at her, astonished. Correct! It had been a funny dream.

He did not give her an answer, and began to eat.

At the same time he thought about his dream.

His brother had been walking with him. It was in a city, sometimes it also looked like a village. The butcher had talked a lot, and often spat noisily like he did when he was half drunk. As they walked through the streets he shouted something now to this person, now to that. "Well, old customer, here too!" or "Morning, colleague, wait, fellow, you bought me out of oxen!" or "Stop, stop, Thresel, you little witch, where are you off to so fast?" The butcher knows everyone, acts familiar with everyone, is good friends with everyone, and mostly talks about business whilst they rattle the money in their pockets.

"Leave off the stupid talk!", he had said to him.

His brother looked at him with venomous eyes, they shimmered green and got bigger. Soon afterwards he saw a snake crawling out from him. The further it squirmed, the more dwarfish his brother became. Now he had entirely vanished, and the monster hung in the air in front of him. It was moving towards him in wavy lines with its mouth wide-open. Now it darts at his chest, and buries its fangs in him. He looks around fearfully for help, but he is suddenly in a forest and all alone. He wants to cut the snake off, but his arms lie impotent. He cannot move them. And the snake is feeding on his heart.

Then he screams in fear, and wakes up.

"That's it, I am half a man, torn up, withered up internally. Why was I a fool? But he talks so well, asks so nicely, acts so abject, so ... so ... so ... entirely truthful, like a snake — yes, yes, dammit."

Then he springs up, and begins to wander back and forth in his room, half-dressed and shuffling.

He looks dark and threatening, bows his head and wants to think further ... oh, his brother is yet more, yet much more!

But he makes no progress. Rhythmically like his steps it constantly goes through his head: a — sna–ke — yes — yes — dam–mit.

Always the same!

And so it goes for half an hour in brooding monotony.

Then it shoots up in him again — oh, my brother is yet more, yet much more!

He stops, and begins to brood again.

But in its strenuous urge the wall clock prattles confusingly, and he hears the clock again, regular with the swing of the pendulum and endless: a — sna–ke — yes — yes — dam–mit.

At first he is interested in the words, in hearing the old thoughts in a quicker tempo.

Then for him it is already as though the clock is speaking the words. Then he does not want to hear it anymore, and again starts to roam stomping. Yet the more he walks the stronger the ticking seems to become. Finally he flies into a passion. The eternal prattle of the clock almost puts him out of his mind.

Now it is preparing to strike, whirring, and it seems to him as if it is laughing mockingly. Then "clang" it strikes one. "Rogue" he hears and then again: a — sna–ke — yes — yes –

Then he emits a cry of fury, falls to the floor, grabs his stick and strikes the clock from the wall so that the dial rolls around the room.

Now it was deadly silent in the room, only the coal fire chugged and sobbed. It was as if someone was crying apologetically. Over what? Poor engraver! –

"Quite right!", he thought with childish schadenfreude, threw his stick in the corner, and sat on the chair, supporting his head in his cupped hands. He moved his right foot back and forth, looked at the shadow it made flickering back and forth, and thought of nothing.

"Jesus Maria!", cried Therese on entering.

She bent down, lifted the mainspring, examined it for a while, and then pecked at the dial with it.

"Aha, it has struck!"

But, how had it come down! Then her eyes become big and appalled. She folds her hands full of pitying anguish. Then, however, with the quick murmured prayer, "God be with me!", she sidles timidly and tremulously to the plate, and doused the roast. Then she walks backwards to the door, always keeping the dully brooding man firmly in view.

Finally the door handle falls creakingly into place, and she heaves a sigh of relief.

"So, then! good Joseph! This is dreadful!" She didn't like pronouncing the word, but she felt it boring into her good, true, loving heart.

"I'm going now across the dark hall and down the black stairs, across the bright street, over into the dark house. Night, light, and more night again, that is life. Everything is perishable", she philosophised.

Yet before she could step into the figurative sunlight of life again, she clenched her fist.

"And if you are still looking so peculiar, the cobbles aren't getting twenty Marks!" A mouth with a walrus moustache rumbled these words from on high to the frightened ones below.

Therese was a spinster and childishly shy in front of men outside the house, and now she was pressed by such a torment.

"Oh God, oh God", she gave him the slip.

"Won't you throw your arms around me", growled the man stomping upstairs.

"Damn!", he groaned halfway.

Someone had once said in public that he had a pot belly. From then on he had played the fatman and suffered terribly under the proud burden.

"Six morning pints", he wheezed on, fingering his body. "In three years, if it continues like this, I'll have to have an apartment at ground level. But always better than a drylander!"

"Good morning, Josef!"

The patient tore his face from his hands, and looked with empty eyes at the arrival.

"Don't you recognise your old friend, Klinke?"

Klinke ... hm — hm — the flickering memory slowly, mechanically came together. He always drinks eight glasses, has a bicycle, an ugly sweetheart, a new blue-striped suit, and a large moustache.

Then Schramm started swinging his feet again.

"Ha, ha, a nice business that!", Klinke threw himself onto a chair.

"I tell you, it's been unbearable! sure! The old looker is away, you know. He's sitting warm now off the wool he's shorn off us and the boss. Could be it was a fellow with whom you could talk and — everyone ultimately having — when it comes to the crunch and the master is sleeping — glue on their fingers — naturally everything with dignity. Sure! The old dwarf, the good skin.

We're good as not getting a dwarf! — When he goes past, he nods and winks to you like a maid to a calf as it is being led to the butcher. 'Poor animal', she wants to say, 'how does that taste? Mr Butcher has another hand when he says "Hey!". Yes, yes, and you surely thought, nothing will happen to me, ha, ha!' Truthfully, so it occurred to me. What do you think, Josef?"

He had stopped swinging his foot. What did he probably want?, he asks himself, and remains silent.

Klinke waited for an answer, but he did not receive one. That's why he looked inquiringly at the patient.

"You! — are you all well? Will you be up and about soon?", he motions with his head to the glass engraver.

I know you, fox, worried Schramm. He has only come to convince me that I'm not able to work anymore. Then he'll run off and ingratiate himself into my job.

I know you! And he nodded with his head a few times like a branch swaying in the wind, swinging up and down, slower and slower, weaker and weaker. I know you, fox!

These thoughts lay as far from the questioner as the suspicion had earlier lain from Schramm's childishly innocent character.

Cheerfully animated, the talkative visitor began again.

The Engraver

"Yes, yes, just come, you understand. Or, if it'll take a bit longer then I'll pack my things and march to Lusatia. The devil wouldn't stand the work. Always just shells, lines and onions! Dammit, why was I in Berlin? Perhaps to receive the same work as a cuckoo now! Of course you earn nothing with that rubbish, and even when you bend over backwards. And I tell you something, like I told the master the other day, if I don't get different work soon, master!, I said. 'Let it be, if Schramm is well. I hope by the way that he will return soon. So many pieces are ordered by Russia. You can't get them finished alone.' So, right, old punter, you're over there again tomorrow? Then it'll all be well again!"

"When I lift such a finely engraved vase from the wash tank and see the floral threads, the buds, leaves and tendrils, then — truly — then it'll be to me as if I am looking my little one in the face. Isn't it so, Josef? You know, of course. I don't have to see your face. I know you. When the others burst with joy, you always simply make big, happy eyes, and press your lips together. But inside you are happier than everyone. What's with all the praising of the master? nothing at all, rubbish! I know them all! They see only the engraved things, but of the art, not a trace."

Schramm had leant back, and was looking angrily at the ceiling. With Klinke's last words he thrust his right heel against the floor, and spat. "Nice art that", was its meaning, "when you muddle an entire sentence! Windbag!"

"So you're coming. Shake on it!"

Alright then, dumb ... Then I don't need to say anything, and Schramm gave him his hand without blinking.

"So, now it'll be everyone for Holy Week. I need fifteen marks of wages for beer. Of course, if my navel was on my spine then it would be gone. But then," he struck himself on his belly, "but then! It is my wife, my piggy bank, my sweetheart, ha! ha!" He broke into exuberant laughter.

Schramm's face, however, was getting paler, and he riveted a venomous and disdainful look on Klinke.

Oh, you scoundrel! I know you, hypocrite. But you're not wrong. And he bit his lips to keep his boiling agitation from making a sound.

I'm not laughing, I'm not, and if ten such ... were to come like you. Abusive names were not familiar to him, hence a doubled fury raged in him.

Was he always not yet wanting to go then? I know he will force me to extremes, and then everything will be lost. Then he will become the first. I will then be able to go and sit in the ditch.

Who needs a mute?

The Engraver

It was the first time that he owned up to his misfortune. The terror and anxiety over it was growing and threatened to overwhelm him. But he didn't tear himself from the terrible thoughts over it, rather his quaking soul was looking with brooding indecision into his horrified face.

Who needs a mute?

And before his mind's eye the images of such misfortunates appeared. They wander in tatters, rest on the verges, sleep in barns. Adults turn away from them, cold and indifferent, and children caper around them, tugging at their coats, making faces and splaying their fingers.

Who needs a mute — it weighs on his chest like a crushing blow. His breathing quavered and his shaking hand sought his hot forehead. He covered his eyes with his fervid, dry hand. He didn't want to see his misery. But blue, red and yellow globes danced and flew through the night before his eyes. In each there was a face, and each face was contorted as though in painful struggle. The mouth of each one alternated helpless, ungainly awkward expressions. He saw how the faces were striving to speak. But it was in vain. In vain his full, tortured heart begged his paralysed organs. In vain the unmuffled spirit coerced it with bitterly defiant will. It always lingered for the word at the mere onset and the desperation only showed in his eyes. The agonising martyrdom of the soul was becoming visible there. So I am ... so ... so ... so ... he chased the dancing patterns with miserable attention into his self-created night.

It was as though he was dying.

Oh you human soul, how easy the sunny strokes of fortune frighten you, and oh, how misery crushes you deeply. –

The engraver's hand fell from his eyes as though his arm had been hacked off. –

Klinke was in a jovial mood and swayed tottering back and forth in the room. He demonstrated the "new walk of the velvet monkeys".

"So — always mincing with the heels like a tenderfoot, the elbows — ha! ha! — like, ha! — like the bowl hooks on barber signs. — Over the big toe, with the head wagging like a polar bear, the back bent like a basket woman. You, Schramm, and always: a–a–a — day — Lord! – I'm a different fellow this evening!" He began exuberantly to bellow "the beautiful Adelheid", stamping and clapping his hands.

The merriment felt to Schramm like a mocking of his misery, and his desperation dissolved into a deep, nameless sorrow. He rested his damp eyes pitifully on the man springing around, who had just begun another waltz, "Polish". His arm movements illustrated the lilting melody, and his fingers grasped at the tones in the air. However, they complied in no way with the rhythm, but followed paths reaching from his belly up over his head.

As Schramm followed with his eyes the swinging around of his colleague, he had a thought. With the mouth you don't need to work. Legs and arms are still sound. Thank God. The legs? who knows!

He sprang up and measured the room with long strides. –

It really was still like lead was in his legs, and with each step he felt a slightly painful inhibition, but in fearfully quaking defiance his will asserted itself over his weakness. He must walk! and he walked. But he could not calm down yet. What use are legs when the calmness and assuredness of his hand is gone! We'll see.

He lifted the mainspring of the clock up and held it calmly between his thumb and index finger.

They quivered.

Darkness passed before his eyes. Oh no, it can't be. My eyes and agitation are guilty. "Nonsense! My hands are as steady as ever." — He threw the mainspring aside angrily.

And tomorrow it starts again.

Complete embarrassment and dedication came over Schramm. The smallest thing irritated him. He would most of all have liked to have walked over to see his position. He looked forward to tomorrow's day like a schoolboy at the beginning of the holidays. He looked for his work clothes and examined them closely. All buttons were sound, no holes, no loose threads, all pockets intact, everything as it had to be.

Then he fetched the sheets of artwork from his chest of drawers. Studying them had been his Sunday treat. Today they would be getting him ready for the following day. He began — for perhaps the hundredth time in his life — to view the first sheet, then the second, the third, and so on.

Here and there lay variations or new designs executed in his own hand.

As a rule delight seized him as he viewed the sheets. The beautiful forms were uplifting and warmed him in the same way others feel great and pure after reading a sublime poem or after apprehending a deep plane of thought.

This ideal trait had vanished in him. Hate, vanity, mistrust, suspicion: they had not left him in the past weeks. He, with the warmth of his heart, with his generosity, his childlike purity and naivety, had reared them in dull brooding. They were his negation. Vacantly, mechanically, hastily the thoughts followed one another.

While he was now examining the sheets with morbid attention and turning them quickly, only one thought existed in his soul — just laugh and pull faces. When I have placed the first finished jug next to me, you will turn to see that I am still the same and you will bend your backs.

Hm, a trifle! My head hasn't suffered at all!

Now comes the "Rococo Pattern".

He closed his eyes and turned over — correct! And now "Bacchus" and now "The Piece of Fruit". With flying haste he turned the pages. Everything tallied.

"I am the same fellow! Ha, ha, you ass!"

He winced. A heavy dull noise struck his ear. He had gotten loud in his excitement.

Oh! The thoughts foaming with rage in him have burst out, and the rabble has heard it! –

He knew that it would come to this. Of course! wailed inside him. That's why he sits so quietly.

He was becoming unconditionally addicted to every hateful, mistrusting thought and felt a sort of lust in the pain it caused him. Of course he knew it would come to this, and yet he had no proof, he still had not looked at Klinke.

We'll see!

He endeavoured to crease a featureless face and let his eyes wander peacefully in a wide arc after "The Lovers in the Forest". When he looked over at the head of Klinke, his glance flew, lightning quick, sharply hostile over his face. And then he forced his attention on the image in the corner.

I thought so, he wildly developed his thoughts further. But thus far keeping his disguise, thus far! Such a nasty, evil fox. But I am something cleverer, little friend. Should you also turn pale, open your eyes wide and stare fearfully, and fold your hands sadly and pitifully, yet you will not be able to swallow the mischievous lines around your mouth. No, little friend, now the comedy is over, now you must leave — leave — leave!

All these actions were making a quite different impression on Klinke.

He had watched Schramm's apathy and brooding indifferently, "... he is always like that, and hears and sees everything." He had acted out the "new walk of the velvet monkeys" in the expectation of making Schramm laugh.

In vain! That annoyed him. He felt socially defeated, and he was used to winning, always had laughter on his side and — nothing gave. In the end he found it boring, and got ready to leave the room.

When Schramm, however, sprang up after his cry of inner joy, "and tomorrow it starts again", sought out his clothes and examined them, then the curious, scandal-addicted visitor sat down again and thought expectantly, 'a funny old fellow, you have to say that. What will happen now!'

Now Schramm was leafing through the artwork. At first he turned the sheets gently, careful and earnest.

"The old dealer in trifles!"

The Engraver

Then the sheets flew quick and ever quicker. How they rustled from right to left. Schramm's eyes opened and closed, fearfully tense earnestness and grim anticipation alternated with a smile becoming ever wider and more exuberant.

Klinke was astounded.

Then he was squirming inwardly with laughter.

"Utterly insane! utter! ha–ha–ha!"

Then suddenly a deep throaty sound like the roar of a stag rumbled over Schramm's lips.

Klinke started at the sound.

Fright seized him, however, when he observed his friend's face. It was now rigid and unmoving in pale horror and terror. Suddenly, however, all his facial muscles are falling into quick, mad movements. Now his mouth is widening and wanting to smile, but his eyes bury themselves venomously. Now quiet earnestness is working its way up, closing his mouth and smoothing his forehead, but his cheek muscles remain taut. Earnestness, dignity, fury and forced friendship scurry across his features in a confused dance.

The impotent endeavour to show something else is driven quickly away and gives his facial expression a fearsome fixity.

Now the struggle is over. But even now it is only a dormant antagonism. One watches, his face shall look indifferent and — rounds into sweet, devious geniality.

Klinke felt a stifling horror.

"Oh, he is wild!"

Jesus! Now the flashing, stinging eyes are resting on him, skipping away, returning and drilling and attaching themselves, venomous and full of hate.

"He is wild!"

In fear for his soul Klinke begins telling jokes to bolster himself up. He speaks effervescently of "the fat pastor's cook", of "the catcher and the ray!" and of many others. He recounts them full of haste. After each joke he breaks out into whinnying laughter, and then his words swirl monotonously over his lips again.

But Schramm fully grasped his horror with threatening eyes, and didn't release him for a moment.

Now he must leave — leave — leave! —

I know, he thinks, his mercurial nature cannot stand the calm, steady, attentive look. At the same time, however, his eyes burned in anger, rage and scorn.

Finally Klinke rose. He must have worked up all his "courage".

"So tomorrow, old man, adieu!"

Schramm heaved a sigh of relief,

See you, you scoundrel!

The departee paused on the stairs though, wiped the sweat from his brow and murmured,

"The utter idiot! And totally mad as well, totally, for sure."

He spat scornfully and continued walking.

"Well, the colleagues sitting in the tavern will be wide-eyed when I tell them everything and — the fun tomorrow!"

"Yes, I wouldn't exchange marriage for a million ...", he whistled as he turned the corner.

The Engraver

String beans for lunch? They're cheap now!", old Therese asked.

Schramm nodded mutely and drank his breakfast coffee. Then he strode to the window.

Earnest joy lay on his pale face. The firm decision had stopped the welling and surging in him. He saw his life lying in front of him: a long, straight, unattractive path. But the bright light of a firm plan of life shone over and in him.

He looked out the window.

The world of summer lay in front of him like a voluptuous woman awakening.

In the blue eyes of heaven the soft clouds of her recently flown night dreams still lay. The fresh day glowed rosily on her cheeks. Across her bust lay the dark coat of forests. From her corn-golden hair the colourful wreath of meadow flowers glowed. From a thousand birds' throats the sweet forward-looking dreams of a just awakened, new life surged through the endless edifices of the universe.

Not clear, dark, veiled, but in spite of that these thoughts surrounded Schramm's soul more colourfully and voluptuously.

You beautiful world! It climbed in him and was caught as trembling tears in his eyelashes.

He felt delivered, resurrected from the dead. The terrible thoughts and dreams which his brooding induced were giving way like ghosts. From an immeasurable distance they surreptitiously squinted at him from their shadow eyes.

What would he have come to, had he continued lending his ear to his misanthropy? — You have to pull yourself together. You must not become addicted.

He folded his overcoat and fetched his watch from under his linen shirt.

"Six o'clock! Now I'm going for a walk until around half past six, and then I'll report to the boss, and I'll already be at work before the others arrive."

He walked in the direction of Ebersdorf.

An unmistakably daunting feeling drove him into the open air.

How will it go? he asked himself. God, if only the first piece that the boss looks at is successful, then I'll be the old me. But, if it is a failure, what then? –

The doubt didn't want to leave him.

The water grumbled and sobbed below the high bank next to him. He heard cheeps above him in the crowns of the pines. A light wind carried the sound down to him.

He felt daunted. He wanted his thoughts to stop. But the more he struggled against them the louder and more oppressive they recurred.

Then it struck half past six and he turned around.

He turned towards the path which lead to the factory. It went uphill. Schramm felt himself weakening. But he did not moderate his step. He was shaking at the possibility of having to pause worn out. Finally he was there, the glass-works lay before him.

He turned around, took his hat off, dried his sweat-soaked brow and gauged full of satisfaction the distance which he had put behind him in twenty minutes.

... Tomorrow it will already seem easier for me. Oh, it will go alright ... His doubt didn't want to be silenced.

Slowly he began to resume his walk. Then he paused again. Multiple bangs, clanks and crashes were coming from the glass-works. The glass makers were blustering and commanding in every key. The factory youths were laughing, singing and whistling. Carts were creaking and jarring. Glass overflow was leaking out crackling. Coal carters were slapping and swearing. Horses were wheezing and whinnying. The locomotive was hissing and spitting. Children were skipping, load bearers were slinking past stooped, women were carrying their children in their arms. Over him the cable way's coal wagons were purring in endless series and making a loud racket when they passed the bearers.

Everywhere dashing, hustling, bright, loud activity. He listened and watched everything avidly. Contentment and certainty came over him. This was his world. Here he had grown up, here he suddenly found everything again, his childhood, his youth, his whole life which had lain buried for weeks under the shadows of a monotonous passion. And like a child after a solitary walk breathes joyfully again at the sound of his siblings in the nursery, so too did the animated, humming life around him again make him steady, brave, hopeful, at peace.

A loud crack startled him. A coal wagon had plunged from the heights and lay wrecked next to him. Workers came running and took away the the coal and the wagon. As they went away he heard them saying,

"It won't run again. Smashed completely in two. It's completely over for it."

The other wagons were continuing to hum above him. The full ones ran down groaning, the empty ones danced clinking along, each to its destination. And over in the yard and the blackened drab houses, the confused shouting, jarring, clattering, whistling, grinding, and running back and forth were merely the heartbeat of a big, strictly regulated whole. Everything was striving to the same goal. Everything followed the call of duty, and everyone was jovial and full of pluck.

The measure of fulfillment of duty is the measure of human happiness and greatness.

And me? Schramm looked at the place where the coal wagon was wrecked — — — me? —

Everything went its way, had its destination, its path and goal. Men, women and children were running confusedly all over the place, and yet they were close and interwoven — the strength sustained the skill, the languid quickness helped the clumsy force, the tender painfulness curbed the raw haste — everyone was connected and growing inwardly and they felt whole in their common mutual dependence.

He, however, to whom faithful work and fulfillment of duty had been everything — pleasure, sport, rest, peace, love — everything, had to stand apart, abandoned, idle, alone, unhappy.

What would he think about if he was not permitted to work anymore? — What would he talk, read, dream about? —

His soul had become homeless.

What did he still have then, but his misery ...?

Then a leaf fell from a tree.

The wind lifted it and swirled it downwards, led it over flowery meadows and — threw it on the path under the hooves and wheels. — It had once been green, lisping in the spring breeze, laughing in summer and swishing in the storm — now it was wizened and orphaned. In the dust was its grave.

And me? –

Schramm staggered backwards as though hit by a numbing blow.

Then he walked onward stooped. –

With trembling, throbbing heart he headed for the factory owner's house. He had seen him coming and now stepped towards him.

"Good morning!", he greeted the sorry one. "You're here again finally." He had reached for his hand, and shook it gently.

"Even the Russians are waiting for you, ha, ha!"

Schramm's soul was suffering from the contrast between his condition now and that before as he stood opposite his strong, confident boss. He felt so wretched and incapable, even of living.

He stared sadly in front of himself for a while with big eyes. Then he riveted them imploringly on his boss's face. Klein felt the mute cry of pain in Schramm's eyes hammering at his heart.

"Now, my friend, chin up! No engraver works with his tongue if his arms and legs are sturdy.

And they're okay. No, no, you're the same old and so am I. So — and now go to Mr Binder and have him give you the designs for the fine vases."

Schramm bowed, and turned to go.

"Yes, what I wanted to say as well, no one has been able to find your brother yet. You will probably be summoned by the court some time soon."

The engraver shook his head slowly and cooly. He wanted to forget it. Clemency and forgiveness reigned again in his soul. No, no! He rushed himself, he thought, he is so good otherwise. He is probably gone. My misfortune is penalty enough for him, my misfortune and his conscience.

Klein misinterpreted his shaking.

"Now, your brother was seen with you on the day!"

Then the thought came to Schramm that it would be impossible for him to stand opposite his criminal brother in court and ruin him by giving evidence. — He mustn't have been! — And now he was shaking his head energetically in answer to his boss's incredulous exclamation, and looking at him steadily. — Of course! You wouldn't be able to meet anyone else in the eye if it were made out that your own brother is a killer. No, no! —

"But, I can't understand you!", called Klein. "Now, if you don't want to say it, your brother will have to do it! Apart from that everything remains as it was between us."

They parted.

... as it was ... the engraver's heart sang without end as he strode on.

And now he was becoming addicted without reserve to the joy of reunion. For him, who had not deadened himself through drinking, passions and sexual debauchery, an abundance of friends and beautiful, stalwart memories also lay in that smallest of circles.

He enjoyed them in broad leisure.

His childhood had prospered in the wide squalid yard. Oh, back then the sky was so near, everything big, beautiful and most blessed so easy to reach. The whole world so small, and his small heart so big, so big and his childish soul so large and omnipotent.

Oh age of youth, oh age of heroes.

Schramm paused in the middle of the field of his boyhood.

From ash heaps, high mountains of glass remnants; from grey, decaying walls and blackened windows the images of his happy childhood climbed up and told him sweet, joyful stories.

He listened silently in bliss.

"Good morning, Josef!" Old Jogwer was carting a load of fireclay from the glass factory over the wooden bridge and greeted him from a distance.

The Engraver

"Good morning!" He stopped next to him and stretched his calloused hand towards him.

"I've been looking around for you for ages!"

Jogwer had been a childhood friend of Schramm's father, hence his familiar attitude with the engraver.

"My God, can you still remember? We last saw each other on oath-taking day. Ten weeks, yes, yes, a whole ten weeks. Jesus, Jesus, you were so completely wrecked and gone because of your brother. And, my God, if your father were to rise from his grave! August, that rogue of a boy, has to go and do something like that. But I have always said it to my wife. Marie, I've said, August got nothing from the Schramms. You can say what you will, it happened, he came into the world under an evil star. I knew it, God forgive me for my sins."

Jogwer fell silent, and looked awkwardly circumspect at the engraver from his aquamarine eyes.

"Where did he attack you then? Couldn't you escape him?", Jogwer listened. "What?", and held his tin out to him in encouragement.

Schramm took a small pinch, but made no noise, and made no gesture.

"There where the stand of larches begins, hey, was it there?"

"What? did not you feel or see anything beforehand, that he was up to no good?"

Schramm wanted to wipe the memory of his misfortune absolutely from his mind, absolutely, with force. He laboured to think of something else — yes, there by the wall I had flown the big kite with Anton Strangfeld.

"The people say it was a rectangular bottle that he hit you with!"

... It was as big as I was. The paper was from — um, from whom then! — How you forget everything! — He half listened to the old man. Then he assailed his memory again ... It was blue and white paper. Anton had provided the line and I had painted the face on it ...

"I just can't understand that you didn't grapple with him. Did he come so quick that you couldn't seize him?"

... Oh yes, it climbed as high as the chimney.

He had been half listening again. The memories of the attempted murder surged like a dark wave. Struggling against it, he answered the talkative old man's last question in his thoughts, torn up, sure enough, discouraged. Sure enough, but the devil probably knows how it came ... no, and — he clung on to the picture in his memory — then he turned to the Oberberg. It remained hanging on the lightning rod ...!

"Haven't you heard anything from the authorities yet?"

Now that was enough. –

He shook his head, and walked away.

The Engraver

Jogwer watched him, "He isn't quite right yet!"

The women's gossip must get in my way now too, Schramm thought as he stepped onto the wooden bridge that led into the glass factory.

The grim creases were showing on his forehead again already, around his mouth the ailing features were digging themselves in, and his eyes were beginning to seize everything, drilling and blazing in terrible splendour. His soul, however, was floating in vacant indecision. Attracted by this dismal image, but ripped back by bitter will and hastily thrust into the beautiful past, it swayed upwards mechanically like a day labourer to the light of the golden age, whilst in its hidden centre a quiet, inexplicable force was yearning for the hell of the patient's bed and convalescence.

With trembling and vexation Schramm felt it becoming stronger and grasped for a straw to deprive his spirit of the whirl of thoughts and the probing of his relationship with his brother.

He had turned to the side and was looking rigidly at the ground. For a long time he could not find anything.

Eventually the memory of his father's image had flown in front of him. It had hurried there shadowy quick. The loving, wrinkled face did not want to turn to him, nor to help rescue him from the evil thoughts. He sadly contemplated it.

Then it rolled dully behind him. When he turned around old Jogwer was looking him in the face. For some reason a wizened, pitiful smile lay around his mouth.

Lightning quick the thought sprung up in the engraver's head: like that, father used to smile just like that. Oh, and then the loving face was standing in front of him with the same anxious smile which exposed the long yellow canine on the left side.

"You shouldn't worry yourself so like I do", the good man had said, just like old Jogwer today, meeting him on the bridge. "That's why you must put your shoulder to the wheel, and if you have the gift, then you'll measure up too. Now I must keep tempering until the gravedigger puts me in the ground." The little Schramm had intended then, "to measure up".

With fearfully trembling attentiveness and awkward embarrassment he now brought his entire course of education to bear on himself.

It had to rescue him from the acrid, irate brooding over himself and his current position which was gripping him more and more. It had to force him sideways into the normal trajectory of his old life. It alone was able to unite his powers to the first important piece of work.

"Oh God, if it is a failure, what then?"

With throbbing heart he grasped the image of himself as a schoolboy which just then fluttered into his memory. He saw himself going into the factory for the first time. Blue shirt, clogs, a cloud of tousled mousy hair under his cap — a dead-ringer for all "factory boys". Yes, that was him! He compelled himself to his joyful surprise and stepped with this memory into the middle of the factory's din. –

A youth clattered over to him, pushed him with the rod on which he "was inscribing" a finished, still white-hot "Parisian" (now even lampshades were blown), laughed broad and loud, and whistled to the annealing furnace.

You beautiful time, where are you!, the engraver engaged his blood in precious sentimentality.

But then his soul's abyss gaped wide. His other, grimmer, wilder, more persistent spirit ripped open his breast with a crushing wave of sighs, "Ha! and what would I have become? And what can I become?" A calm muted furious oath ripped the red colouring from his face.

But what use can it be, he checked himself straightaway. I'm not learning to talk by that. I must forget it, I must ... must ... must ...

And shaking with excitement he ran into the thickest crowd.

There he scudded his knees against a boxcart filled with opaque glass pillars. The worker was following it from the annealing furnace. The bump from the engraver made the mountain of glass vibrate.

"Dammit!", cried the worker, "where do you want to go? Sit down and bake yourself a pillar on each side of your backside, sir!"

Schramm puckered his mouth clumsily and in a businesslike way like a doll with a laughing mechanism, and stormed onwards.

I must forget — must — must –

But already a fist was grasping his shoulder, "Boy, if it weren't you, I'd belt a rod over your cap. Rattling my baking again for nothing!"

Schramm stretched his hand out to his school comrade, and laughed distractedly.

"Now," the blower grouched angrily, "you've pushed my frame off course."

"Oh," said Schramm with a hand motion, "for that, if it's just no more!"

"Of course, but a stranger sat on a shard outside, that I know. — Well, we're getting old, right Josef, old friend. But truly, I've worried about you. They said you had been mad for weeks. It took a bit out of you it seems. But the colour is coming back."

The glass maker related bellowing a lot — a lot. Schramm wasn't listening to him, but toiling in his memory.

... It is a good thirteen years since I was a bulb maker. Yes, I already had a position at seventeen. The others, they were all sheep. They had to blow bulbs for four years. Right — and the factory boss always called me the young master — yes — yes –

This pride came very seasonably to him, and he knew to immerse everything in bright, glaring light, to make the most magnificent colours for everything, and to serve himself a sweet obliviousness for a few moments.

"... Well, we are old friends!", the blower weaved into his shouted monologue again.

"I would think, Josef, we were inspecting how a litre looks down below, you have to stretch one out!" His voice droned, and his face beamed that he had finally reached the hazy point of his grand oration.

Ha, I thought so! Oh, the drunkard! Well, I know you all! One just like the other! hissed the evil demon inside the engraver. That goaded him on, and when he had the carousel, a new cooling apparatus, explained to him his second grim spirit pushed past his vigilance with the terrible exclamation — August could cool off his bones there in the glowing wagon.

Schramm observed much more, went here and there, was addressed by many. But it was in vain, he remained distracted. His collectedness, his business-like disposition to work, which he had wanted to enhance on his walk through the spaces of the glass factory, was, barely risen, broken in two by derisive, bitter revengeful thoughts. — On the way to the draughtsman, Mr

Binder, he convinced himself from memory that "his hound of a brother" had only feigned drunkenness, that he "had wanted with decided intent to kill him" in order to "swallow in revenge" the life insurance payout.

He rolled many more dark, angry thoughts hastily through his soul, he raked and raked in the abysses of the heavy hatred which penetrated right through him, but which his slow temperament never magnified and induced into a glowing flame, into clear resolve.

While he was aimlessly walking in the yard and around the buildings, the initially high surging drive of passion disappeared in him, after he had cleaned away from his weather beaten spirit the painfully stiffened, morbidly alive will and from his heart the arduously won fortifying interest and the refreshing, healthy memories.

His defeated soul was empty, dull, lacklustre and doubly slack, his poisoned doubly poor heart was cold. — His sense instruments worked quickly and lightheadedly and yet bore nothing inside.

He saw everything, heard everything, even the most minor. And yet every excitement was so weak, went so quick, was so singularly inconsequent that no feeling, no idea was formed.

The Engraver

He roved like a sleepwalker, but without one's confused, colourfully animated inner life.

He had already been standing for quarter of an hour before the steam producing works which raised water from the pit, and he looked for perhaps the thousandth time at the piston rods pushing up and down, but he wasn't bored. For when the piston went down once again, the earlier impression of the same had already evaporated and Schramm saw with pristine, mechanical attentiveness the glittering of the lustrous iron and heard with surprise the groaning, gurgling and splashing of the water.

He would probably have stared witlessly for a long while yet, but a call snapped him out of it, "Well, Schramm, do you already have the designs in your pocket or are you resting first?"

Mr Klein stopped in front of him.

Schramm didn't grimace.

Like a tardy draught animal is set back in motion by the call of the wagoner, so the engraver turned again to go.

His boss's earlier request lay in him, and worked like a bestial, blind driving force.

... Now he was knocking on the draughtsman's door.

"Come in!", it squawked from within.

He entered, and stood, swinging his cap in his hand as workers do.

In the long room a hunchbacked man on a high swivel stool crouched stooped over his work before him. He didn't look around, didn't once stir, when Schramm entered the room. He seemed turned to stone. Only the whistling breath indicated that there was life in the kinked man. The whistling became stronger and quicker. Finally the agitation burst out into a short whining fit of coughing and then,

"Thunderbolts! Good morning, Mr Buffalo!"

And suddenly the little man spun around twice so that his legs flew sideways, hopped down, and in the next moment was standing under the engraver's nose and flinging an irate "Ha!" in his face. Then he stepped back, spread his legs, pushed his gold framed glasses up tight before his eyes and propped his hands on his hips,

"I've been plagued for years by this bandit, but it hardly makes a difference. There is always another who can't button up his coat over his coarseness. Dammit! How often do I have to say it then — I am not your one of your kind! I am not an artisan, I am an artist!" (With that he was blowing mightily.) "Understand? And I demand respect. Yes!"

After that he strode diagonally across the room to a cupboard.

That was Mr Binder!

The Engraver

Schramm thought he looked like a clown and had to laugh.

"It is impolite to laugh at a superior!" — Binder intoned the word in speech marks.

Schramm's slack spirit began to stir — "a nice superior" — and his heart was catching life.

The smile didn't want to leave his face.

Mr Binder looked at him for a while inquiringly. He was apparently waiting on a rejoinder, and already had something rude prepared.

The engraver's mouth remained mute.

Oh my God, Mr Binder now remembered, the mute, yes, yes, with the tidy brother!

Then! — It's not worth a word.

"You should," he began business-like in sharp, loathsomely overbearing tones while he was walking to the table and waving Schramm over with an imperative hand motion behind him, "You should engrave vases here according to this pattern — but hold true to it. You will never learn to understand the spirit, the rousing soul of the artwork. You will merely inscribe it, copy it — like a real — genuine ar–ti–san."

The engraver's brow clouded over. He took the designs from Mr Binder's hand roughly. So, that'll show you, it was meant to say. He then looked at the drawing attentively. It portrayed a large, tastefully arranged bunch of flowers over which three small dancing nymphs floated amusingly on butterfly wings.

A magnificent drawing in fact! Yet he is a devil of a fellow, the little nipper! Just the beautiful rosebuds and above it the little fellow in the billowing veil as he looks at the flowers avidly! ...

And suddenly he was feeling it welling up voluptuously in his breast — the foreboding, the dreams, the animated thoughts came over him just as they had seized him that morning as he had watched the awakening world from his window. He found there in the drawing a deeper soul admittedly than Mr Binder had conceived. The latter, however, felt flattered by the long inspection, and now began in benevolent schoolmaster tones, "The three graces are faith, hope and love. On the left above the branching rosebuds is love. The veil is frivolously slung around the luscious body and shrouds its charms. The lascivious look is directed at the swelling rose which represents, i.e. symbolises, the awakening sensuality. – Symbolism is the most important thing! Rembrandt was quite right there, if I also condemn his penchant for the ugly — condemn I must!" — And the midget genius drilled his glass eyes in the air and glared at the giant towering in front of him as though at a schoolboy.

"In the middle hovers faith", he again took up his explanation after he had smugly rested on his bundle of laurel for a while. "— faith. Serious gestures inform its contemplative soul. I wanted actually to give it a prophet's beard to indicate the origin of christian belief, but ..."

"Thra!"

The engraver snorted appreciatively. It had sounded like a trumpet blast.

Binder stared at him. Fury and rage made him blanch. With quivering lips he screeched, "Such impudence! Here — here — here — no — you do — such a thing — here — that you elevate yourself. Thunderbolts!"

The outburst of fury didn't make the least impression on the engraver. While he slapped his cap against his leg and turned to go, he thought, a superb design, but difficult! That meant keeping the chin up. Otherwise ...

His indifference drove Binder to extremes.

"You are a rogue. It's a lie, a stinking lie! Your brother wasn't thinking of hitting you at all. You were drunk, and then ..."

Schramm stood rooted to the spot.

The entire weight of secret fury was rolling onto his chest. His heart and lips were trembling. He turned around energetically to "stand up to him for once". — But you were left for dead! — Grumbling, dull noises swelled over his lips, and his eyes flashed in grim, spine-chilling fervor.

Mr Binder leaned lifelessly against the table, and screamed for help with all his strength. But fear was clenching his chest, and so it sounded like the whimpering of a young dog.

Schramm spat in his face, and slammed the door behind him.

Mr Binder slowly returned to normal.

He wiped his face, and when he had cautiously looked out the door, and determined that the engraver was already gone, he balled his fists.

"Just wait, birdie! You think the branch on which you are sitting is green! Just wait, just wait, when it is sawed it will die off. We'll see. No! — it drains the colour, such a lack of respect!"

The Engraver

So that too! — If he said it then it must be what people are saying! — The engraver walked, pressing hard against the wall, along the smoky building and finally turned into a door that stood open. The threshold and the hall tiles were well-worn. The plaster was flaking from the walls in parts. Packed straw lay all over the floor. On the right a door, on the left another — and so on — each like a beggar's coat: patched, abraded, sometimes too big, sometimes too small, hanging askew, closed fast and yet loosely ajar as every lock on them was damaged. The doors creaked, groaned, rumbled, sprung open and closed as though corrupted by the noise and movement around, next to and above them.

On the right a door — on the left another — a long corridor. –

Schramm paused for a moment before each one, like a load bearer compressed by the weight of his burden.

"Go in! — — — — no! — am — I though — — an ass!" — the mechanical labour of his soul expressed itself. Deep down though it was digging and drilling like an attack of fever: so that too! — after everything! — Me dishonourable! — You eternal God!! — It must reduce me — or crush me! But — what to do?

He walked further. — On the left a door!

"Go in!" — He paused! –

What to do? I will sue the dog! Yes–s! — But the man speaks like a market jew, and me? — Nonsense! Then I have to tell everything in fine detail! No, no! I am being too good there, spreading everything out in front of you, you miserable child. And ... justice? — Ask high heaven! ...

He walked further. On the right a door!

"Go in!" — He paused. –

"No — mangy cat — I'll smack you over — strike you dead — you deserve that, you to whom the honour of another is as dear as your hump. Strike you dead!"

But then the thought came to him that he also knew others who were as terrible and base as Binder — strike them dead! The poison kept eating away — where — how many good, honourable men were on the earth? None — strike them dead! — every one, all the vermin.

He, the executioner, and in front of him the whole world — away with you! — Everyone a head shorter! — Strike them dead!

He burst out laughing: loud, shrill, cutting.

It sounded like the cry of someone drowning.

The Engraver

His heart though was beating against his breast as if it wanted to burst open its bony prison in order to get away from these grim, hellish thoughts.

Schramm pressed his hand against his chest as if to calm it. Then he heard the design rustle in his pocket.

He had entered a dark staircase. On the right the firebrick stamper, on the left the engraving hall. –

"It won't work! — I'm flustered! — Even if it works out — and — what then?"

The noise to the right and the left stretched his thoughts out further and gave him the answer.

From the engraving hall it was screeching and hissing dizzyingly like scornful laughter.

From the firebrick stamper it was swelling like dull, monotonous, languid hammer blows.

It was to him as though he heard fate hammering the coffin of his future.

He shuddered.

In this agitation I *must* ruin everything. It *doesn't have to* be today. He turned around and wanted to go.

"Stop, friend, you haven't been fed!" It was Klinke. He came from the engraving hall and was in his sky-blue monday-suit.

"I had my birthday today, then Czernoch, then Mann — here's the heart's lubricant!" He held a huge "rectangular" full of schnaps in the light of the corridor.

"Sociability! Always comfortable, that's the main thing. Ha, ha! well today's great! Brother, and now you have a birthday!"

He had been pulling Schramm up the stairs. With his last words they stepped into the etching room.

A choir of wavering voices cried,

"Hello, birthday boy!" — Amidst which was heard the admiring call, "Klinke is a right old dog! — up with Klinke!"

Everyone sprung from the worktable, a table made from hammered together boards which ran the whole length of the hall with the exception of the wall with the door, and they arrayed themselves in a semicircle around the arrivals.

Schramm thought to himself, they're all drunk. I think I should leave them, otherwise they'll get worse.

Klinke took over. With droll ceremony he passed the bottle to Czernoch, "Here, my marshall's baton." —

"Colleagues, comrades, friends! Yesterday we celebrated Moltke, the big silent one. Today we greet a small silent one ..."

"Bravo! Bravo! More!"

A dig at his wordlessness, Schramm thought, and blanched.

The Engraver

"He has survived a night-time battle. He almost succumbed to his wounds. But he has won. — I almost had it as close yesterday. I stumbled over a stone and – bloodied my knee. Of course I could in no way smash my head in. For that I'd need two four-in-hand cart loads", he pointed to the rectangular bottle that Czernoch held, "under my hat."

That's aimed at me! — Rage began to build up in Schramm, but Klinke continued steadfastly, "Well, what did I want to quickly say. So, he is well again. He is as it were of ... he is as it were of ... he is as it were new born. The Lord has shaken his hand. Binder has opened his door to him ..."

"Well spoken! Magnificent!" cried Czernoch.

"We are happy that you are here again and want to douse your birthday, and you should open up your pockets and let the rain out. We're still all the same old — Czernoch, the buffalo, Mann, the moth and skirt-king, Strangfeld, the bible moth ..."

Everyone roared and stamped, "Bravo! Klinke, you dog!"

"The others," he continued, "the others are our acquaintance Esau without an E!"

"Oh ho, well, well!"

"And you are still the hindquarters of the boss!"

"On that hee will squeeal inn pribate ...", growled Czernoch.

"Up with Klinke! Up with Schramm! Up with the birthday boy!"

Schramm threw a look full of hate at Klinke, broke free from him, and stepped over to his work station. His miserable distrust had seen vicious "malice, insinuations and insults" in Klinke's every word.

The cutters looked at each other questioningly for a while. But when Klinke nodded with his head inclined to Schramm, and with a wink said, "not quite bonkers", everyone burst out into neighing laughter.

Only Strangfeld, the bible moth, a giant with legs which seemed twisted out of a towel, moved aside. This crudeness cut deep into his heart. He probably had in his clearer, collected inner being an idea of the misery in Schramm's soul which kept faith in the world and God only by the trembling consciousness of his own honour, but which was otherwise veiled by the shadows of grim passions which it wanted to smother and yet bore in painful lust. –

He went to him and pressed his hand with a silent, affectionate smile. Schramm pressed it ardently, oh if he could have freed his afflicted soul and exclaimed, my friend, my saviour! Instead he pressed it again so wistfully that Strangfeld wanted to cry out. –

The rest of them had been sharing the "rectangular", clinking their glasses, and singing:

The Engraver

"Free the art
and wide the throat,
always without a sorrow.
When there is no gold,
you wealthy world,
you must borrow, borrow!"

"Leave the coward, I'll put in a mark myself too!", screamed Czernoch as they finished, and threw in a mark.

Strangfeld beckoned Schramm, made the motion of rubbing coins with his thumbs and drew his mouth up in ironic archness. It was meant to mean, "Give, you will have them off your neck earlier and faster." Schramm nodded understanding, produced a mark, and Strangfeld bore it to Klinke, "To the president of sociability, here's something from Schramm for the birthday drops." Hardly had Mann seen the mark than he too blew a fanfare through his hollow hands, and his eyes flashed.

And then the whole mob arose and voiced a toast:

Refill, and take glass in hand,
Take a deep, German slug.
Long live Schramm and Czernoch too,
By old, traditional artists rite.

Up, three-times up!

It had already been sung many times today with names inserted as appropriate. It was well beloved. For their "artists" charter had not specified holding a tune. Hence everyone used this toast to express their musical credo. Each one was deeply convinced that his melody was the pure, manifest truth, and sought to do it credit by the greatest exertion.

This one was a friend of melancholic ballads. He sang the toast like a funeral march. At the same time he spread his arms sideways and flapped up and down like a stork before taking off.

Another loved the trifling. Ludolf Waldmann was his ideal. Although metre and rhythm didn't tally, he sang the words obstinately according to the melody *My Beloved's Blue Eyes*. At the same time he tapped his knife on his glass zealously and with a sagely blissful face.

Klinke always put himself in the starting pose at the beginning of the toast. But then he sang it according to the regimental march of the eleventh. He marched around the hall, rolling his eyes like a conquistador and swinging his arms like his "blessed bandmaster".

Czernoch was a musical guerilla. In his melody were all the melodies of the world, in each tone all the conceivable tones had a rendezvous. Sometimes you could hear the roaring of a lion, other times it sounded as though someone had trodden on a cat, and then again the far off rolling of a wagon with brakes open.

The younger ones limited themselves to banging the big or small drum with their hands according to the extent of their intoxication.

Everyone, however, agreed that the magic of the toast would have been considerably reduced if everybody had not stamped their feet to the rhythm with the vigour bestowed in them by God.

Klinke had, as if it could be any other way, arrived with the last words in the midst of the singers and had stamped the last "Up!" violently on the floor with a thundering "Stop!", as he, turning in a circle, intoned the national anthem.

After the ragtag melody had just faded away, these noble sounds!

> Brother, give your hand to federation.
> This serious hour of celebration...

Admittedly it left the impression that you were seeing a king clothed in all his pomp dragging his ermine drunkenly through the backstreets.

The participants, however, creased their faces in earnest nobility. Tears ran over their cheeks. One even sank under the table from the emotion. Since they all came to an abrupt end to their knowledge of the text with the beginning of the second verse, the song dissolved into a polymorphic, mysterious humming and finally fell silent entirely.

But then every eye flashed, and like the battle cry of rampaging warriors it bellowed out:

> Whoever has sung the song, a slug belongs to you,
> With the infantry, with the cavalry with'em e'er a brew!

Thump! They all hewed to the table and emptied a glass in one go. The "rectangular" had exhaled its alcoholic soul, and Klinke set out to get a new one.

The Engraver

A youth had carried the vases to Schramm at his work station. Strangfeld gave him a hand with the preparations for etching. He moistened the abrasive in the basin, and arranged it. Schramm laid the leather belt over the fly wheel, and secured the "dampened mat" over the disc.

"Good luck!", wished Strangfeld, and offered him his hand.

Schramm smiled without faith and without hope, and pressed the offered hand trembling.

Then he looked to the departee, for a long, long time, full of yearning. He would have preferred to spring up and hurry after him. He had so much to consider, so much to overcome. But his dreamy dithering will, his inability to decide, the thought of the scorn of his colleagues, all held him on the stool, although he felt completely incapable of work.

His inner being had been completely torn apart by Binder's comments and the taunting ambiguous words of Klinke, the pigdog. The splitting apart had begun with his misfortune in that narrow cutting. One part of his life, his childhood and adolescence, was sinking like a stone, wizened and ravaged, without connection to him and his fate, without awakening any interest, deeper and deeper. All the warm, light, colourful, beautiful thoughts and feelings were leaving him like the birds and sunbeams and flowers all vanishing with the dying summer.

The other part of his being, the most recent past, was welling up in him like an early, dusky autumn evening. Storm, frost, emptiness, night and death were its children.

It suffused his breast, his entire being, and with it returned the grim spirits which the glorious morning and his courage had frightened away: mistrust, hate, poverty of hope, the ghosts of dead self-belief and faith in humanity.

Oh, and his soul was not floating in doubt anymore, was not looking hopefully anymore into the abyss, into the distance where the beautiful times and their bright companions had vanished.

A weak ecstasy, constantly trembling in death, a pale notion of doubt from blessed days was all that the uncorrupted human past had left behind in him. His soul's reaching for the beautiful domains of memory, its agonising certainty of living death in the event of constant separation from them, its struggle for the bright, spiritual existence which it had fought before the coal wagon on the cable way, against Jogwer, in the glass factory, all this lay in it like a mechanical, blind force, had reached the resolution to repudiate the world of thought and feeling, in the present in any case, in order to return to the lost paradise. But the engraver did not see the path he had to take. He pushed his soul in blind struggle into the wild commotion of his inner being.

And it settled in and took up residence in the rubble, with death, in the emptiness, and it clothed itself in coldness. –

The entire outer world flew past it quickly and shapeless like the wind. Nothing was more pertinent to it than what was connected with his hatred of his brother and everything arising from it.

Otherwise it turned, an atom amidst millions of atoms, with the cycle of life's waves. Now it was standing quietly and everything else was flying past it. To everything outside it presented the features of its face, the content of its inner being.

Fear of annihilation of his physical existence was the only thing which connected Schramm with his fellow brothers and which made his behaviour outwardly similar to theirs.

But his will was so enervated by spasmodic brooding and fruitless dreaming that the entire struggle now ensuing for the assertion of his place was nothing but the mechanical, wrestled fulfillment of a decision which was pressing darkly, hard, monotonous and as though from a distant age.

The long prepared metamorphosis in his inner being was finally accomplished so quickly, that Schramm felt the weighty, wretched changes in himself as one notices the night's end, even if it isn't visible to us. — Minutes passed and it was accomplished. —

Schramm had meanwhile averted his face from the door and was staring out the window.

"But now I have to start", his slack, work-shy will stirred itself.

Slowly his foot sought the treadle, the wheels began to purr idly as though irritated.

But like the rotten invalid raises his sunken heroism, like late autumn sunshine, at the sound of war ballads, so the former love of his profession stirs in the engraver bit by bit with the long accustomed sounds. But it lay more in the muscles, as these produced the personality's cohesiveness through their habitual movements. These intensified and grew in apparent inwardness as though the higher senses were drawn into the old craft-like activities.

And as the engraver now looked attentively at the design, a vase in his right hand, an undivided zeal for work seized him.

He "fed" the disc from the abrasive basin and his hands introduced the vase confidently.

The Engraver

He moved it up and down and turned it in circles. Now after a short contact he let it skip away with the disc, now it trembles on the fast circling disc: stems, leaves, fruits, flowers come into being on the blank glass as though by magic.

Warm repose, soft joy, comforting certainty filled him more and more once he had obtained the conviction, after wiping off the glass dust each time, that he had succeeded "magnificently" with the work.

"Ha, ha, the same old! That is superb!"

In his eyes awoke a soft shimmer of the happy life of his past reviving.

Enthused, he continued etching.

***

The hall had emptied itself. Everyone had gone. Nobody worried about Schramm. He had expelled himself from their community by his old zeal for work. Everyone watched him full of sympathy and voiced dismissive, irate words about the "conceited striver and conformist".

The most infuriated was "Czernoch, the buffalo". His raw character, his indolence and scruffy work had already put him out the door once. Schramm's advocacy with Mr Klein had obtained a pardon for him. Schramm had done this to prevent Czernoch's old mother from being unhappy, as she received a meagre, bitter charity from her son. But just this generosity was reason for Czernoch hating him even more. For he convinced himself into believing "Schramm has ingratiated himself with 'the boss' just to have himself a pile."

Czernoch's blind hate was a fitting confederate for the affronted Mr Binder, whose snorting vindictiveness was insisting on the swiftest retribution. He had met Czernoch in the corridor after the incident with Schramm, and dragged him into his closet. There the shrewd, devious "artist" stooped so far as to close a pact with the cutter for Schramm's ruin. Czernoch invested his raw violence, Binder his cunning. He wanted to wangle Schramm's position for "the brave, honourable, diligent Mr Etcher" if the attempt succeeded. But in truth he did not think at all of "upgrading" the "rough dolt". In any case he only wanted to have the "crazy toad", the mute, off his neck.

***

Schramm had just finished the bouquet and was looking restfully at the successful work.

Then excited mutterings suddenly filled the yard, rolled down the corridor and up the stairs to the etching hall.

The engraver promptly set himself to work again in order "not to come into contact with the drunkards". The three allegorical figures floating over the flowers still had to be etched.

Just then, as the door flew open crashing, the disc again dug hissing into the glass.

"Of course, if everyone was an ass like that, then everyone could exist on a starvation wage!", called the foremost of the etchers tumbling in while he pointed at the man bowed over his work.

"Eh, leave the coward, that is no man of the future, he has to coat his mouth with honey for the boss again after lazing around for thirteen weeks and stealing the money from the sickness fund!"

"Peace, comrades, that's beside the point!", Klinke reminded them whilst he extracted himself from the tangle. "It is only a question of by which means we in the lawful way, and it is sacred to us, with our just demands ..."

"Aye, aye! and then the boy carries on as if we were nothing at all, absolutely nothing at all, the ...", roared Czernoch.

"Peace! Peace! Hold your mouth!", cried from all sides.

"No, hey, hey, that would be evidence, if I weren't able to tell the truth to the rogue!"

"What do you want then? I ask", Strangfeld approached him threateningly.

"It doesn't concern you at all, I'm not talking to you!"

"Czernoch, if you have something against him then let it be until afterwards, settle it with him alone!", Klinke called out, looking out for his fame as an orator.

"No, and again no! absolutely not, everyone should hear what sort of fruit Mr Headetcher is!"

"Then let him, let him! Czernoch speak!", the accomplices he had just bought off in the tavern called out.

"Finish, Czernoch, finish!"

Schramm was working so that the sweat dripped from his brow, but his face was cold as marble and the drops like ice. He was working with half an ear, half an eye, half the feeling in his hands. His soul and his heart straightened up slowly, trembling under the interdiction of a terrible suspicion. His climbing agitation expanded his chest to breaking point and hung on his faltering breath.

Czernoch's words were tearing him into the maelstrom.

Czernoch was repeating in essence Binder's malicious, unfounded suspicion, but with the difference that his hate and fury piled up a filth of horrid profanities between the isolated sentences.

"It's known," he continued, "everyone knows, brother rogue, that you have f---ing lied. In your wild temper over a few dingy marks which your poor brother had hid — hid away, merely taken out of circulation! ... In wild temper over having lost a few dingy marks, you wanted to strike your poor brother dead. But gentle brother had quick reactions, had hit you on the head despite the pastor! ... The lie is that your brother had wanted to strike you dead. You are a rogue for sure! You, damned skinflint, have your marks again, you know how to skim too. Feed your face, you robber bandit!"

During the final sentence the listeners had heard a hissing singing.

"It's burning!"

The vase lay in Schramm's hands as though it had grown. He had succumbed, and it was as though he had turned to stone. His feet worked as though in spasms. The "mat" was dry. The disc was cutting so that sheaves of fire sputtered. It had long since dug a hollow. But Schramm wasn't paying any attention. His head lay slack on his chest. His lips twitched and trembled. From his motionless, wide-open eyes silent tears were slowly falling.

"Feed your face, you robber bandit!"

A mark coin flew at the vase clinking. Schramm broke out of his trance. His work was totally ruined. Streaks, knots and hollows were strewn mazily over the vase.

His life annihilated! — His honour gone! — The respect dead. — — The faith had died. –

He, a beggar — an outcast — despised — oh! — — — — — — by a scoundrel, a drunkard! –

His anger was incensed — in mad rage he sprang at Czernoch. Strong arms grasped him.

"Hound! What are you saying to me? I gave my last cent to him so that I became poor as a beggar, and you dare to accuse me of payback and attempted murder? You are worthy of being strangled. And you, you senseless drunkards who laugh about my misfortune, I will seek him out, my brother. Heaven help me. I will seek him out. I will bring him here before you, and make him tell you why he struck me half-dead. If there is a God in heaven then I will succeed! You, however, Czernoch, you beast, you will die!"

So screamed his soul. –

But from his mouth spurted wails, gargles, hisses, rattles. His lips trembled, his mouth foamed, his eyes stared straight upwards, his face was distorted, his body quivered.

Two men held the raging man with difficulty.

"Don't you see that he's crazy?", someone squawked. Binder, the hunchbacked dwarf, emerged from the mass, the smile of sated vengeance on his unattractive face.

When Schramm saw him, he broke free with superhuman strength, rushed at him, and laid him out flat with a tremendous punch.

Then twenty hands grasped him, and the next moment he was lying outside in the corridor.

He remained lying for a while dazed.

The Engraver

The beating of the firebrick stamper brought him around.

The restless timbers thundered dull and slow so that the floorboards on which he lay trembled.

His future grave was ready — he lay in it, but alive. Oh, he could have died, then it was all over, all forgotten, all that was ahead and dancing monotonously, raggedly, swirling through his head. The seething agitation, the savage life and storming in his inner being had run riot then for good! —

When the unfettered flames have consumed a house, they will probably flare up again, but then they sink down for good and die under the ashes.

The rip in Schramm's soul which had been getting ready for so long was accomplished.

His past, his human existence had foundered. His soul still lived in blunt, bestial hate and the stone-hearted stupid decision to seek out his brother. He had forgotten the original reason for both, or they had become so meaningless that he could not think of them anymore. He also didn't know anymore what should happen if he found his brother.

He just hated him and had to seek him. That was the entire content of his mental life.

A life worse than death.

The timbers were continuing to beat dully.

Seek–ing ... seek–ing ... it rammed the blows misshapenly through him.

Under this interdiction he stood up and walked uncertainly down the stairs, along the downstairs corridor, across the yard, the street, always further, further — where to? ... seek–ing, — seeking.

He neither looked up, nor looked around. His view was fastened to the ground. He strode across the fields to the Wolfkoppe forest. The wind was swishing in the pine needles, it sounded to him like: seek–ing — seek–ing.

The chirrup of the redbreasts, the husky call of the jay, the delicate wooing call of the tit, the mumbling ripples of the little forest stream, they all sounded identical to him.

Restlessly it pushed him further, always further ...

Finally it was becoming evening.

Exhausted, he sank into the moss and was soon asleep.

***

Fate had ravaged the house with fire. The timbers were destroyed, the remains of the walls crumbled and toppled, into the open hatches, the empty rooms, into the secret underground spaces, destruction dwelt everywhere.

Lower yourself down, eternal, eternal, gentle night!

Oh, that the morrow never awakens over the ruins! Else the poor owner must despair. –

The Engraver

The sun already stood quite high. A hooded crow on the tree under which the engraver lay let its prolonged, croaking cry ring out, then it chuckled hoarsely a few times whilst spreading its tail feathers.

The sleeper was startled, wiped his eyes and slowly raised himself up.

"A crow, hm, hm!"

He was almost rigid from the cold.

Cold, cold! he shivered all over. Then he stood up and looked around. A dark feeling of surprise at finding himself in the forest stirred in him.

With languorous steps he walked straight through the forest. Then, as though from ambush, the thought suddenly assaulted him,

If "he" — his brother, of course — met me here! No stick, no stone, the path a long way off, people nowhere! — Carefully, fearfully, he peered through the trees. He stood still and listened. Nothing stirred. Quietly he slinked to the next hazel bush and broke off a stave. — So! —

It was now sloping steadily down. He took the first path he encountered. He peered alertly to the right and left. If he heard crackling, he stood still and gripped the stave tighter. He had no other thought.

... Then there was a rustling, rolling and singing. He was standing by Schlegel's churchyard wall. They were burying a dead man. A requiem rang out.

"A burial ... many people?" ... He peered over the churchyard wall ... "dammit!" — ... and quickly cowered down again.

"I can't walk along the street. Then everyone would see me. I must get past the dog, past the front of the brewery ... he could be siting inside there and see me. Oh, and the other people," he mused further, "they are all on his side. Before I look someone will have put it out that I am seeking him and — shoo! He has vanished. That means being on guard!"

"Mr Schramm, was it you then? Are you unwell?", a compassionate, female voice had suddenly called over to him. He started up, but sunk his head quickly back into his breast.

"Oh, the 'Wagners'! Such a group too! What to do?" He ruminated for a long time. Finally it came to him like an epiphany. "I will pretend to be crazy", and he sprang up, struck at the wall with his stave, and muttered darkly.

The woman had been waiting a long time, and had asked him a few more questions that he had not heard. When she received no answer she had become scared. That's why she had quickly stepped back. She was looking around just as he sprang up and belted the wall with his stave.

"My God, my God, he is crazy!", she said to herself in horror, and turned right towards the main road full of terror ...

Schramm realised that he was not wearing anything on his head.

"That suits magnificently. When people see me without a hat, then they will think, oh, he has been with so-and-so and is now going home. Then there's still time to talk to August, who is sitting at the brewers or somewhere else. — — But it's cold, dammit. I'm going home, I have to fetch my cap. — Through the middle of the village — there I can play the observer. — I'll see in the people's faces whether he is there — !"

A narrow, steep path led down from the churchyard wall to the main road, which was also the village street. He took the path and was soon on the wide, bustling road.

Holding the stave in his right hand, looking sharply and conspicuously at the passersby on the right and left, he went down the street dragging his feet. His back was chaffed, dirty, covered in moss and scraggy grass. His hair was a mess and hung low over his forehead.

Everyone he knew stopped or timidly avoided him.

"Truly, he is crazy!", was whispered first here, then there.

Schramm though was thinking, "Like I supposed. Of course he is here, why else would everyone need to avoid me? Even Frank — his best friend once — passes to the side. They are all in cahoots. But just wait, I will find him ..." Soon he was standing in front of a smoky, unadorned house with many windows. He entered the filthy hallway and climbed the familiar creaking stairs. He found his apartment open, however he was not astonished, but went in and threw himself on the first chair he hit upon. He felt absolutely exhausted.

Something rustled behind him. His eyes remained shut. He did not stir. He was so exhausted he did not want to suspect anything.

Now the sound of soft footsteps was becoming louder. He turned around fearfully. Therese stood behind him, paralysed with terror, and raised her wide-open eyes at him. Next to her was a pack in which various articles of clothing lay. She held the coupled handles in her hand.

Finally she ventured to speak, "Mr Josef! You're very pale. I must leave. My sister is sick. She is alone and doesn't have a carer. And — and — for the last three months — I have given — my wage — which — I want to — I have already. You are so unhappy. — Adieu!" — She could not hold herself any longer, she sobbed and snivelled, and held out her hand to him.

"Good bye! May God be with you."

Schramm had let go of her hand, and was giving her with a blank look.

Then she stepped through the open door. "God be gracious with him!" She went down the stairs unsteadily as she could hardly see the steps through her rolling tears, the good, faithful soul.

Schramm made a contented face, "Alright that she's going. I must sleep. I'm tired, far — too — tired!" –

He lay down still clothed on the bed, and soon fell asleep.

Suddenly he felt an arm seize and shake him.

"What are you up to there, Schramm?" The landlord, a square-built man, was standing in front of him. He was fashionably dressed. But on his feet he wore tall boots which pushed out the covering long trousers at the back, and in his face lay a brutal, cold aspect like people risen from the masses wear and which strode for years over ruined existences and desperate hearts from which it remorselessly sucked its criminal gains.

"Today is the first!", he began angrily with even harder voice when he saw that the engraver remained perfectly blase. "You can't stay here anymore. Why haven't you given notice on time? Don't you know when the first is? The money, I mean the rent for the past three months, is also still owed by you!"

Schramm looked at him irritably. But he did not make a face to reveal it. He merely thought, "Now the ass wakes me up, and I was sleeping so well."

"I probably could have guessed that you would have none!", the landlord continued after a pause. Then he looked around the room, and cleared his throat.

"It is sixty three marks. In order to spare you all inconveniences, I will take your furniture as payment. I don't want to do you any harm." In silence he calculated thirty marks profit. "You can keep the glass things. I don't want to profit from anything, other than what's deserved!" –

A shrewd smile leapt onto Schramm's lips. The glass things?! Oh, you dolt! I'll take them and go hawk them off, then no devil will guess that I'm looking for August. Good — good!

All the tiredness immediately disappeared from him. He sprang up, fetched a large hand basket from the corner and began to clear out his commode. Ornately engraved beakers, vases, bric-à-brac, glasses, he packed them all in straw that he extracted from the bed and laid them in the basket.

The honest landlord followed all his hand movements so that nothing else was slipped into the basket. He went from one piece of furniture to another, stroked and fingered everything lovingly, registered the value, and added it up.

Meanwhile Schramm had finished, taken his stick and hat, and stepped out the door without heeding the landlord or looking around.

The landlord locked the door. The bar slid across. "Settled!", suddenly fell from his lips joyfully.

"I didn't need to say so many words after all. He understood nothing though, as he is obviously crazy. But it is better that way, really, really, that is the main thing. Form must be kept. Now nobody can be a bother to me."

He had reached the front door, and was whistling jovially, "Don't you see he's coming?"

"Where will he probably go?", he asked himself as he watched the engraver hastening up to the village.

"He shouldn't actually be left to run around. He could go to pieces as it were. But better stay quiet, hold my peace. The community would bleed me again for such a wretched subject. Run off, I have my things!", the noble philanthropist ended his murmured monologue, burst out laughing, then whistled again the polka he had broken off and turned towards his apartment with leisurely steps. –

Schramm meanwhile hurried onwards. He stopped in front of an old, wooden building which looked out grouchily on the street with its small windows and he looked up. "Karl Marche's Brewery and Public House", he read, and nodded contentedly. The church tower's bells announced the twelfth hour just then as he crossed the threshold.

"Slickly, slickly!", he murmured, and sat down at a table in the darkest corner. On one of the tables a small bottle stood, of the type in which schnaps were usually given to inferior people, and a large glass.

"Ha, ha!", he noted suspiciously, a scent. "He" always tended to drink from such bottles.

Mechanically, like in his days of fortune, he grasped in his pocket to lay out the money ready for his bill. In his right was a handkerchief, the left was empty. From his vest pocket he finally dug out a fifty.

In the bar nobody had been seen until now. Then the kitchen door opened. Schramm turned his face. A burly, young, moustached man, an adolescent lad in shirtsleeves and a woman came out.

"Everything empty! A business going to hell in a hand basket!", the older one said. "But not after all! Dammit, isn't that Schramm? Right! Well, where to? What's new? What, a basket? A present inside? Yes, yes! Fine goods?", and he grabbed at the basket's cover.

"Ng, ng, ng, ng!" the brewer heard.

The Engraver

With "fine instinct" Schramm sensed that the "ape" only wanted "to have a look". That's why he took the basket, and placed it in the dark corner so that the brewer could not reach it. Then he pointed to the coin.

"Schnaps?"

He nodded, and would have done so even if the landlord had asked something else. For the suspicion had risen lightning quick in him, "He will be hiding in the kitchen." The woman's smile had encouraged him, that's why he wasn't listening to the content of the question which the brewer had directed at him.

How can he do it so that they don't notice? He drank a swallow, and submitted to his senses. The kitchen had two exits. I can't go through the door there. Then "he" will run out the other, or I won't be let in at all. He continued to consider whether it would not be better to climb in through the kitchen window from outside, but he rejected the plan after some consideration. "So it goes", he murmured, stood up and walked back and forth in the room as if going for a stroll. With that he first struck the billiard balls like a sharp cue artist, then he drummed on one of the tables as he walked straight past like an unemployed musician, whistling and watching those present with a sharp eye.

Finally the woman also sat down at a table. Nobody paid any attention to him. Everyone was preoccupied with the midday meal.

Then a dog barked outside. Schramm ran outside as though curious, closed the door, and placed an empty bucket before it so that "he" would fall over it if "he" wanted to slip away unnoticed. Then he crept listening to the kitchen door. After a few moments he opened it noiselessly and looked inside. He examined the whole room, every little corner, nobody there! He listened for a moment. Suddenly he heard from the bare boards quite clearly — the cupboard is open — clap! — clap! — he is hiding in there — clap! — clap! —

Astounded he looked around for the speaker. It did not enter his head that he was thinking so animatedly. He saw the tin lid of a pot in which something was cooking hopping up and down.

Now it was clear to him, "Knew it of course!"

After a few, thoughtful hesitations he gamely quietly seized an iron bolt hook hanging on the wall and set about opening the cupboard. His heart trembled with excitement, his hands shook.

With the nails of his left hand he forced the door. He was holding the hook ready to strike. —

The cupboard now stood open — old clothes! Searching he thrust with the iron here and there. Nothing there! nothing at all! —

Disappointed he let out the breath he had been holding, and carefully closed the door.

Then it rung out again: clap! — clap!

"Shut up!" — Furiously he sprang, and knocked the skipping tin lid so that it fell rattling to the floor.

The next moment the landlady was standing before him, "Dammit, what are you looking for here?"

"Ng — ng — ng" — and Schramm pointed to his mouth which he moved in a chewing motion.

"You could have said that outside. Nobody has nought to do in the kitchen! March, out now!"

He went out with lowered head. The agitation, the elusive life in him, had quite suddenly subsided. Everything in his inner being was dead again, cold, empty, lacking feeling, night, night.

He sat down in front of his glass, held his head in his hands, and stared at a hole in his table's oilcloth covering.

"Here!", rang out next to him, and a steaming bowl with mysterious content shoved itself in front of him.

Greedily he began to eat. He had taken nothing in for a day. When the woman saw how quickly his trembling hands led the bites to his mouth, she became pensive and saddened. Poor fellow, she thought, such a noble, reputable man half a year ago and now ... oh, and how good he was. Oh, heavens, he didn't deserve it! —

Schramm shoved the bowl across the table and emptied the schnaps glass. Hastily the woman seized it. "He has nothing else anymore from life! So he'll want to drink another!" She filled the glass once more, placed it before Schramm and went with the bowl through the room, which had completely emptied meanwhile, to the kitchen.

The engraver took a deep draught again.

The pleasure of the schnaps brought his blood to boiling. The dreariness in him was beginning to weaken. His soul again began to stir monotonously around the abyss in his inner being.

"He really isn't here anymore. Why did he go away so quickly? He must have noticed that I am on his heels and moved off. He didn't feel safe anymore. Oh, the wily customer has made it over the border into Austria. Someone should look for him there then. But just wait! Surely he has chosen the main road in the direction of Wünschelburg. If I go over the mountain, I will already be there, and when he arrives I'll seize him. But that means being quick, otherwise he will give me the slip again."

Hastily he took his stick, hat and basket and stormed out the door, stumbling over the bucket.

Not long afterwards he was seen hurrying up the steep path of the Kapellenberg.

The Engraver

The sweat dripped from his brow. It was beginning to sting in his lungs. He didn't pay any attention to it.

"Whoever is over the border, nobody will find him, he will be as good as if he was in Cameroo — Cameroon" — — — the words went uniformly, hastily through his head to the rhythm of his steps. —

The Engraver

What the engraver had expected of his future many months ago had become the terrible truth, had become reality.

Now he was wandering in tatters, resting in ditches and forests, and sleeping in barns. Adults turned away from him, cold and indifferent, and children capered around him, shouting and tugging at his coat, making faces and splaying their fingers.

If he could have been his former self, mute admittedly, but in possession of a need for love, the craving for happiness and unclouded, general attention for his true human welfare and the processes around it, then the contemplation of his condition would have driven him into the arms of despair.

But now he was not noticing the change which was proceeding within him. The entire world around him wore the countenance of his thoughts.

The consequential egotism of his hate ensured that the colourful many-sidedness of the connections of his soul to the outer world was

remoulded into grimmer, immutable uniformity.
The many eyes from which the human soul sees
the animated, multiform and multicoloured flow
of the world were closed. Only the glowing,
hidden eye of hate measured everything outside
him according to the unworldly standard of its
soulless laws. And when the hate had dissipated
the last sparks of warmth in the soul and heart
into barren, pedantic plans and suggestions, it
itself disintegrated, dispersing its morbid
collection, it became purely bestial and flowed
into the organs which were wearing its tyranny
down in monotonous service, and its old work of
destruction continued there. Only sometimes did
the alcoholic spirit of the schnaps still give him
his old strength, and it hurried into his brain,
into his soul and whipped his thoughts up in a
wild whirl and enfeebled his body in disorderly,
aimless agitation and work. Then the engraver
declined the schnaps glass crying and stormed
out, whether it was day or night, stormy or
snowing. In wild, breathless running he rushed
to the next forest and chased after shapes which
his vindictiveness led him to believe in. Suddenly
they would stop as though rooted to the ground
in terror, and Schramm, gnashing with fury,
would then belt them with stones and branches
until he sank down fatigued next to the tree by
which he had seen his brother or Binder.

The Engraver

On other mornings, when frost and hunger tore him prematurely from his hard bed, his empty, dead inner being affected an inexplicable, clinging dread and fear, he felt that somebody who had walked all his life with him, been trusted by him, was gone. Then something like a deep worldly desolation pressed on him.

He had learnt from experience what he was missing and how he could help himself. He assiduously amassed the meagre tips given from pity and hurried to the next tavern.

By drinking two glasses of schnaps his old companion, hate, was awakened and it murmured to him the old profanities and stories, and Schramm felt himself again.

In such a state he once walked through a village. A transport wagon stood in front of a blacksmith's. It was equipped with two horses. One was being shod. The driver was holding the leg and the smith was trimming the hoof. The other horse stood harnessed in front of the wagon.

Schramm stopped and watched. The hand movements of the smith and the falling nail shavings entertained him.

Then next to him it rang out raw and ragged, "We have just come from Bohemia. — We stopped at some inn. There we were able to look into the lounge as well."

Curiously Schramm observed the horse that was still harnessed. It raised its head up, shook it so the brass rings whirred, and then opened its mouth again, "In a tavern on the border a man was sitting too! He was small and fat, had a blue nose and watery eyes. He drank schnaps and was always looking fearfully into the street. He was probably frightened of someone."

Schramm held back his breath. He stepped quite close to the head of the horse.

But it kept silent, closed its eyes and let its head sink jerkily deeper and deeper. Schramm whacked it on the side encouragingly and murmured incoherent noises, "Continue, please continue! I already know who he is", it was meant to mean. The horse was frightened by the whack, it flipped back the yoke which wanted to fall over its head, and peered at the horse being shod as if it feared being overheard.

Then it raised its head, tore open its mouth, and Schramm heard the piercing cry, "It was your brother who you wanted to strike dead!" As the engraver heard his thoughts cried out like that, mad despair overcame him. As though defending his life, he struck the horse with his foot, belted it with his fists and gurgled and cried, "Cursed beast, you're lying, you'll die!"

The horse reared up into the air, and struck out. The wagoner grasped the reins with his left hand. With his right he seized the whip, and swished it down on Schramm, "Wretched bum, get away. I'll help make you shy of my horses."

"Ha, ha, ha!", the smith laughed with his entire body, "that's crazy Joseph! Always tight, it won't harm him, he rambles around everywhere and makes trouble!"

Schramm fled. At some distance he turned around, balled his fists at the two of them, emitted wild sounds and finally disappeared with lowered head.

Spurred on by constant consumption of schnaps, he now began the hunting of his brother hastier and more restless than before. Sometimes he surfaced in this, sometimes in that village, to quickly disappear again. Sometimes he was seen in the field cowering in a ditch, sometimes lurking behind a tree. Then he was heard again overnight fighting with his brother. Else he was creeping on deserted paths from house to house, from village to village. His eyes flamed in weird fervor, his face bore the traces of mental disintegration. Rutted, waxen yellow, it looked like the image of a fanatical ascetic.

Meanwhile the winter came, early, heavy with snow and biting cold.

It was in the month of December. The nails in the shingle rooves were springing creakily, the snow crunched under the hooves and feet. It was terribly cold. Icy mists crept along the ground, up the trees and remained hanging there as icicles. The sun squinted down at the earth from a narrow crack in the clouds only to soon hide itself away again. It had already been risen for an hour and yet seemed to still be standing in the same place as though it was frozen fast in the sky. No breeze was felt, the trees of the forest stood motionless like giants turned to stone. When the birds flew from the rooves to the barns, they hardly spread their wings. It looked like stones dropping.

The old smith in Reichenau stood on the threshold of his house and blinked outside with wrinkled eyes and lips closed fast.

"Damned weather that! Twenty four was a winter too. But this one betters it, dammit!", he murmured to himself and rubbed his hands.

"Well, what's stopping you? Get into the smithy! Franze is fetching the sled today and Elsner wants the drawbar too. Go! Look when you're finished!", grouched a raw, female voice from within the house.

"You get that in old age", murmured the white head. "Fondness for children is a hundredweight on a thimble. Yes, yes, my holy one ..." He stuck his hands deep in his pockets and wanted simply to "mimic", when immediately behind him came the growl, "Out of there! You'll freeze! If you don't rub your hands in the good times then you'll have to suck your fingers until your cheeks burst. We can't to everything. If you want to eat, father, then you also have to help by working!"

The old man stepped down, and got out of the way, watched after his son, and spoke to himself in philosophical repose, "The children today have heads merely for butting like bucks and mouths for biting like dogs."

Despite these grim words over the coarse behaviour of both his children — old, surly, crooked people — no venom swelled up in his soul. For an argument in the morning, as aperitif or afters with breakfast, counted,, from the first days of marriage with his "holy one" up to today, among the unavoidable scenes in his house. With time the bitterness and severity had become the solitary expression of his soul, even his love clothed itself in it.

"Before you open your hand you should see what you want to grasp, and before you open your mouth you should consider what you want to say. Else you don't grasp anything correctly, else you just speak rubbish. But such are young people. When the heart is full, the mouth is wild. They like to say what they want. Two against one — many dogs are death to the hare."

With this saying almost every time he concluded the observations which tended to start up machine-like after every argument.

Today, however, his temper was really depressed by the foggy, dismal, cold winter morning, and as he opened the tattered door of the smith's workshop his hope-forsaken, tired heart sighed, life is like iron. Either it's glow dies quickly into ashes, or it rots away slowly in the earth. With one it goes quick, with the other it doesn't want to end.

Why must I wait so long!

Then the stooped old man disappeared in the half-light of the sooty workshop, where it soon began creaking and hissing. Sparks flew up, and a small fire looked out with its erratic, flickering eyes at the street and into the fog.

The children going to school saw it skipping and sputtering, saw the swirl of sparks being thrown up and going out, laughed, clapped their little hands and went away amused.

The old farmers who came from the early mass emitted a clear, "Good morning, master!" into "the black smith's workings". Their "elders" elongated the blue tips of their noses to the left. "No, no! Already working! Hard luck there!", their toothless mouths hissed.

The old smith paid no attention to anyone. He indulged himself in thoughts which were no lighter than the dark corner which he had turned his back to.

When he once by chance turned around, the engraver was standing behind him. The old man started instinctively. Although he knew him, he could not withhold a look of horror. His sudden, unnoticed arrival, and the terrible change that had occurred with him called it up. His face, covered up to the eyes in a bristly beard, the pale cheeks deeply furrowed, the forehead wrinkled with folds, the mouth sometimes wistfully closed, sometimes open despairingly, and then sometimes shivering again with cold, the eyes sometimes scrolling wildly and glittering, sometimes fawning timidly and appalled under his brows, in the deep hollows, and sometimes standing lacklustre in the shadow of helplessness and hopelessness. It was as if one were seeing death die. –

Seeking warmth, he had buried his haggard, frozen blue hands in his chest. Oh, no warmth had resided there for years, no life, no light. –

How could the mouth round itself, the eyes wander blinking happily in quiet peace, the heart have fervour, the knees power, the muscles strength? Oh, for years the lips had sucked hunger, the eyes had sated themselves on contempt, the heart had smashed itself to pieces in lovelessness and the delusional living soul had wasted its powers and strength.

So appeared a wretched, lost human life hounded by death! –

The old man let his eyes wander once more from the rag covered feet to the head of the engraver.

"Warm yourself up, warm yourself up!", his withered lips said and quivered.

"We've left the key! We're going to the mill. Take good care and work!", rang out from outside, then a sled scrunched away.

"That's nice!", the white haired iron tamer said to himself, "now I want to get the poor devil warm. It would be better for him of course, if he lay frozen for a long time. But he is human."

Coals flew into the fire, the bellows hissed afresh, warmth and fervour flooded over the unfortunate one who had settled down on an anvil, and the old man made a contented face, "I'll make him warm soon!", and his dull force drove the heavy hammer in slow blows on the glowing iron.

The engraver rocked back and forth so that the warming glow of the fire drove the cold from his body. Then he fell asleep and dreamt — of his brother, of his misery, of his revenge, confused, disconnected, monotonous ... Now he hears the distant dull blows. His eyes stay shut, his ear opens. His soul thinks the accompaniment, seek–ing — seek–ing. Now it roars around him, over him, everywhere, like in the forest. He half opens his eyes. The faces are continuing to swirl through his soul. Through the gauze of his black eyelashes he see the room mounting blackly, and the grim roof is arching above. –

The Engraver

Who is it? He is walking next to him, stooped, tottery. His hands are waving about in the air. It is him, yes, August, the dog who struck his happiness dead, his honour, his existence.

In the wild intoxication of victory his hate tormented soul flies from the fetters of bleak death. The full force of the drabness, despair, vengeance and bold fury of all his thoughts and feelings throws itself on his heart, which is laced up as if by claws of fire.

The shivers of avid excitement leave him motionless.

Now he hears a drunken voice quite clearly, "Mr Engraver is a religious gouger whose gentle 'Our Father' face doesn't make the the devil overlook that he cheated his brother of a thousand marks, and the same thousand marks that he then nobly lent him!" It screams around him, in him, and the sound waves seem to go through his body so that every fibre shivers with the words.

The face awakes wild hate in his soul and continues to swirl.

Now the one standing in front of him is becoming a small, hunchbacked little man who screams, "You are a rogue! It's a stinking lie! Your brother didn't want to strike you dead at all. You were drunk!"

The face awakes his wild hate and continues to swirl.

A strong, square-built man grows from the squat dwarf. "Feed your face, you robber bandit!", he roars and sinks. Now it is sneaking up, slowly, slowly. His forehead is high, white and cold. His grey eyes are staring helplessly, his mouth is open, yet mute, but a sobbing and whimpering goes through the air. Now it is coming nearer! A ball of fire lights up ...

The entire content of the unhappy part of his life has assumed form and is screaming at him in the characters of his torturers. His soul-deep, lifelong misery is compacted into a point and threatens to pulp him for good. But his passionate bitterness, his love of life is also springing up to its full height. Desperation is lending him strength.

The face with the stealthy eyes of a predator is coming closer.

Rogue, cheat, whore chaser! he hears it cry or groan in him, around him, through him.

A fist is raised to strike.

Then in nameless fear of death, paired with wild vengeance he seizes a hammer lying in front of him and — lets it swish down on the skull below him.

Dully, lumbering the image falls down.

In bestial fury the engraver springs at it and keeps striking until his arm has gone limp.

As he senses the body underneath him twitch, as the warm blood trickles over his hand, it is to him as though shadows are flying from his soul, as though a grisly, wild desire, which shrouded in veils was constantly whipping his soul, died in fulfillment, as though a grim dream faded under the gleam of softening light. The horrible shadow world of his inner being goes far, far away. Its hate-filled look does not look at him from afar anymore either.

Then the veil also sinks from his physical eyes, and he sees the true world — and under him the murdered smith with his skull smashed to pieces.

Horrified he springs up and backs away.

"Dead ... dead ...", it comes clearly, quietly over his lips. — "My God, my God ... what? — Blood on my hands? ... What's with the hammer? — And the brain on it? — — Not a dream?! — — Am I the murderer? — m — me? — — why? — — my brother, oh! — my brother!" — He could speak again.

The morning has risen over the ruins.

The unhappy owner must despair.

He has the feeling that he has hiked a long, long way over hollows, through swamps, past abysses, through a desolate, terrible land. And now he is at home with himself again, with his soul, in his heart. But his soul has rotted, his heart doesn't throb to life anymore. The future yawns in front of him like an endless grave. There he must, the living dead must die a hundred deaths if he wants to continue living. But he does not want to, out of love for himself. His life has condemned him to death. He must die. The imperative rests in him. He wove it during his time in the maze, because he believed his honour depended on his fellow men. Now it ruins him. Staunchly he yields to the verdict.

Broken, with swaying knees the engraver trudges into the nearby forest.

That afternoon he was found hung. –

About the Publisher

Our mission is to provide translations into English of the complete works of neglected major European writers. We do not cherry-pick works that seem the most marketable, but rather seek to provide a complete collection of each writer's works so that readers can follow the writer's development and decide on its merits for themselves.